NEW YORK TIMES BESTSELLING AUTHOR
KAYLEE RYAN

Copyright © 2025 Kaylee Ryan
All Rights Reserved.

Without in any way limiting the author's exclusive rights under copyright, any use of this publication to "train" generative artificial intelligence (AI) technologies to generate text is expressly prohibited. The author reserves all rights to license the use of this work for generative AI training and the development of machine learning language models.

No part of this book may be used, including but not limited to, the training of or use by artificial intelligence, or reproduced in any manner whatsoever without written permission of **Kaylee Ryan**, except in the case of brief quotations embodied in critical articles and reviews.

This book is a work of fiction. Names, characters, events, locations, businesses, and plot are products of the author's imagination and are meant to be used in a fictitious manner. Any resemblance to actual persons, living or dead, or actual events throughout the story are purely coincidental. The author acknowledges trademark owners and trademarked status of various products referenced in this work of fiction, which have been used without permission. The publication and use of these trademarks are not authorized, sponsored, or associated by or with the trademark owners.

The following story contains sexual situations and strong language. It is intended for adult readers.

Cover Design: Lori Jackson Designs
Cover Photography: Michelle Lancaster
Special Edition Cover: Emily Wittig Designs
Editing: Hot Tree Editing
Proofreading: Deaton Author Services, Jo Thompson, and Jess Hodge
Paperback Formatting: Integrity Formatting

KAYLEE RYAN

WHAT ABOUT NOW?

MADDOX
PROLOGUE

I'VE BEEN LOOKING FORWARD TO today. Not because I get to hang out with my best friends, who are also my business partners, and their families. Not even because my guy Forrest is falling hard and fast for the single mom of twin girls. And not just because Roman's daughter, Lilly, is getting older, and she's sure to be a ball of fun, and Uncle Maddox is here for it. All of that is a bonus. But today, I'm looking forward to seeing her.

Brogan Pearce.

She's all tanned legs, and big green eyes. Those cutoff jean shorts she's wearing ought to be illegal. Thankfully, I'm wearing dark sunglasses to hide the fact that I can't stop watching her. It's like this every single time we all get together. It's as if I have no control over my eyes, as they drift toward her time and time again.

Just Brogan.

She's all I can see.

Hell, for the first time in my life, she's all I want to see.

I've been around beautiful women. She's not the first, but she is the first I can't seem to be able to look away from. I don't know what it is about Brogan, but I can't get enough . I gravitate toward her every single time.

But it's complicated.

First of all, Forrest is head over ass for her twin sister, Briar. They're taking things slow, but we can all see it: they're endgame. Then you have me. I've never had a serious relationship.

I've never wanted one.

There has never been someone who has come into my life to make me think about more.

Until now.

Until Brogan.

I've been biding my time, getting to know her at the same time as everyone else, but to me, it's more. *She's* more. That's why, as I sit here on this blanket, staring up at the fireworks display, I reach over and link her fingers through mine. It's dark, and no one is paying any attention to us. She stiffens but doesn't try to pull away. I take that as a good sign. I need to remember to do something special for Rayne and River. My little wing ladies who helped me gain this spot on their aunt's blanket.

I'd give anything to be able to hold Brogan, not just her hand. The moment feels right, and suddenly, I have clarity.

I want more, but only with her. I want to know her dreams, her fears, and everything in between. I want her in my arms on nights like tonight, hell, every night. Is this what the guys felt like when they found their girls? Is this what Forrest is going through as he falls for her sister, Briar, and her daughters?

This feeling is intense. Just thinking about us together makes my heart race. I haven't noticed a single woman since the moment I met her. It's just been Brogan. She's holding my hand, and that's a small step, but I need more. I *want* more.

I want her to be mine.

Brogan Pearce is my endgame. She just doesn't know it yet.

BROGAN

MY BODY ACHES, MY HEAD is pounding, and I'm burning up. Why is it so hot? I reach for the covers and freeze when I feel an arm. At least, I think it's an arm. My mind starts racing, and my heart matches its rhythm. Fear grips at my throat, making it hard to swallow. I force myself to take a deep breath and evaluate my current situation.

Not again.

Please, God. Not again.

I take a few deep breaths, trying to calm myself down. I need to get myself together and get out of this bed. I don't even know where I am. How could I let this happen? Squeezing my eyes closed, I try to remember how I ended up here and who I'm with, all the while trying to keep my panic at bay.

Yesterday, my little sister, yes, little... I was born two minutes earlier. It's just facts. Anyway, my little sister married the man of her dreams. A man who has shown my sister and her daughters so much love and patience, it makes my heart happy. Forrest Huntley is one of the good ones.

They got married, we all celebrated, and when the newlyweds went up to their room, Roman and Emerson took the girls to play with Lilly. Maggie and I hung out with Maddox and Lachlan, and that's where things start to get fuzzy.

Opening my eyes again, I peer down at the arm wrapped around me, and instantly, I recognize the ink, and my body relaxes.

Maddox.

Oh shit! Maddox.

I mean, he's better than a stranger, but this will complicate things. Mostly the crush I've had on him since the day we first met. I've made sure to keep my feelings locked in the vault, because what if we get together and it doesn't work out? My sister is married to his best friend and business partner. My nieces call him Uncle Maddox, for goodness' sake. So, yeah, no matter how sexy he is, or how I've imagined waking up just like this, I know it can't happen.

It shouldn't have happened.

I move to try to get out of bed, but the arm tightens around my waist. "Go back to sleep. Too early."

That voice, even laced with sleep and I'm assuming hungover—if the way I feel is any indication—definitely belongs to Maddox.

I don't know what to do. I can't just stay here, wrapped up in his arms. I shouldn't be here. I drank too much and was irresponsible. The last time I let something like this happen—I push those thoughts out of my mind. I'm fully dressed, so that means we just slept next to each other, right? I would know if we did more. At least, I think I would.

I need to get up.

I move again, and he stops me.

"Stay."

"I have to pee." It's not a lie, but it's not the only reason I'm trying to flee this bed and his arms either.

"Fine," he grumbles. "But come back to bed," he says, as he releases his hold on me.

I don't reply as I scramble out from under the covers and place my feet on the floor. The room spins, and I groan and take a few deep breaths. Getting up that quick was not a good plan. When I can finally gain some balance, I move toward the bathroom and lock myself inside.

I don't bother looking in the mirror. Not yet anyway. I'm certain that whatever greets me is going to be a scary sight. My mouth tastes like ass, or what I assume ass to taste like, mixed with cotton.

After relieving my bladder and sitting on the toilet for far too long, I move to the sink to wash my hands. A quick glance in the mirror and I cringe. Ugh, I do not want him to see me this way. Reaching for the water, I keep staring at the hot mess that I am. After I run my hands beneath the stream, I splash water on my face. That's when I feel it.

Slowly, I open my eyes and stare at my left hand that's suspended in the air. My ring finger—*that* ring finger—is adorned with a white gold diamond band.

What. The. Fuck?

I shake my head, close my eyes, take a deep breath, and open them again slowly. The ring is still there. Both hands shake as I reach over with my right and twirl the diamond band. It's a perfect fit. As if it were made just for me.

"Fuck," I mutter.

I don't want to jump to conclusions. I'm sure it was just a ring that I saw and liked. That's all it is. It's not because I'm in Vegas with my sister, who married the love of her life, with a man who has no idea how I long to be with him. The same man I just woke up next to in bed beside me, with a ring on my finger.

In Vegas.

I've never shied away from my problems, and I'm not going to start now. Grabbing the hand towel, I dry my face and quickly brush my teeth before tying my hair back in a knot. Nothing is going to help the hot mess that is my hair except for a shower, and right now, I need to see Maddox. More specifically, I need to see his left hand.

"It's just a ring," I whisper to myself as I pull open the bathroom door and pad my way back to the bed. Maddox is awake, and his eyes trail me with each step I take.

"How you feeling?" he asks. His voice is raspy and thick from sleep, and it's sexy, just like the man, but I push that thought aside. I have more important things to talk to him about.

"Can I see your hand?"

He furrows his brow. "My hand?"

I nod and fight the urge to groan. That was not good for my headache. "Your left hand."

He lifts his hand, and my breath stalls in my lungs. He's wearing a wedding band. It's black and similar to the one I watched my sister slide onto Forrest's hand yesterday.

"What is that?" I ask, pointing at the ring.

His mouth falls open, and then his eyes snap to my hand. I raise it up and wiggle my fingers. "We're married?" he asks.

There's something in his tone of voice. He doesn't seem angry. If anything, he seems... awed. How is that possible? "I think so," I finally answer. "That's the only explanation I can come up with. I was hoping I just bought a ring I loved, but no way would you do the same."

He closes his eyes, and I think my eyes are deceiving me because I swear, there is a small lift of his lips as if he's smiling. "Maddox?" His eyes pop open at the sound of my voice. "Do you remember anything?"

"No." He swallows hard. "Do you?"

"Not much. I remember us leaving with Maggie and Lachlan, and then it gets fuzzy from there."

"Yeah," he agrees.

I turn my head, glancing around the room, looking for anything that might help me remember, when I spot papers lying on the table. My legs shake as they carry me to them. I don't need to pick them up to see what they are. The words *Marriage Certificate* are in big, bold letters at the top.

"Shit."

"What is it?"

I startle at his voice being so close, and I can't stop the shiver that races through me when he gently places his hands on my hips as he looks over my shoulder.

"Marriage certificate."

"So, you're my wife?" he asks. Again, he doesn't sound mad about this or even irritated.

"Looks like it. At least until we can get this annulled."

"What?"

I turn to face him, and we're now chest to chest with his hands gripping my hips. I look up at him. His big blue eyes study me as if I'm a puzzle he can't figure out. "Annulled," I repeat.

"Let's just take a step back. We should shower. We're supposed to meet everyone for breakfast at ten." He glances back toward the bed at the alarm clock. "We've got thirty minutes."

I sigh. "I guess you're right. It's Sunday, so there isn't going to be an attorney open to deal with this until tomorrow, anyway."

"Go shower."

He leans in and presses his lips to my forehead. He's never done that before, and the act has my heart fluttering around like a swarm of butterflies inside my chest. "What about you?" I see my luggage, and all of my toiletries were in the bathroom, so I know we're in my room.

"My stuff is here too." He nods to the opposite side of the room, and sure enough, there's his luggage. "I guess we decided we were moving in together." He smirks. "I mean, that's what married people do, right? They live together?"

"We're not really married, Maddox," I remind him.

"That piece of paper says otherwise, Mrs. Lanigan." The smile he gives me, it's not a teasing smile, but it's gone before I can put a name to it. "Go shower. You can get ready while I take my turn. That is, unless you want to shower together. That's better for the environment. Saving water and all that."

"Nope." I pull out of his arms, needing some space.

"Lock the door."

"Are you leaving?" I ask. Sadness washes over me. I know we can't stay married, but being with him, having his attention, it's something I don't really want to let go of just yet. What happens in Vegas and all that.

"No, baby, I'm not leaving." He reaches up and presses his palm against my cheek. "It's to keep me out of the bathroom. My wife will be naked and wet. I need all the barriers I can get to keep me away."

Oh.

He smirks. "Go. Lock the door," he says again, before dropping his hand and making his way back to the bed.

Quickly, I grab a change of clothes and disappear into the bathroom, and I lock the door just like he told me to. However, the entire time I'm showering, all I can think about is Maddox busting down that door and joining me.

Thirty minutes later, we're both dressed and ready to head to meet everyone for breakfast. Maddox has his hand on the small of my back, leading me toward the door, when I freeze.

"I forgot to take off my ring." My right hand reaches for my left.

"Don't."

I freeze and turn to look at him. "What?"

"Don't take it off."

"So, we're just going to tell them what we did?"

He gives me a stiff nod. "This is my one and only wedding. Let me enjoy having a wife while I still can."

"We're not really married, Mad," I whisper.

"We are. Our names and signatures are on that marriage certificate. It's legal and binding. You are my wife, and I'm not hiding that."

"But it was a drunken mistake," I counter. He bows his head, his chin falling to his chest as he grips the back of my shirt. "Right?" I ask him.

When he finally looks up, his blue eyes are liquid fire. "You are my wife." He repeats the same four words he said just moments before.

"On paper."

"Give me this. We'll get through breakfast. Besides, you're not going to hide this from your sister, and I'm not going to hide this from my brothers."

My shoulders fall. "You're right. Not to mention Maggie and Lachlan were probably there. Maybe they can fill in some of the gaps."

"Maybe," he says, pressing his lips to my temple. "Let's get you some breakfast."

No more words are spoken as he leads me out of the room and to the elevators. There's an older man and woman already on board, and they smile at us.

"Newlyweds?" the woman asks.

Maddox pulls me closer to his chest. "Yes, ma'am."

"Young love." She grins. "We just celebrated our fortieth anniversary."

"That's incredible," Maddox replies.

"Congratulations," I say, finally finding my voice.

"Enjoy it. Marriage is work, but having one special person to spend all the good days, and the bad days with, makes it worth it." The door chimes, and they step out first, and we follow along behind them.

My steps become slower as we reach the hotel restaurant and even slower when I see our group.

"I'm right here, Brogan. You're not alone in this."

"I can't believe we let this happen."

"Come on, wife, let's get you fed," he says, ignoring my statement.

With a heavy sigh, I follow him to the table. He pulls out a chair for me and waits for me to sit before taking the one right next to me.

"Aunt Brogan, you almost missed breakfast!" River exclaims, shoving a bite of pancake into her mouth.

"We said ten, right?" Maddox asks.

"We did," Roman answers. "The girls were hungry, so we came down a little early." He gives Maddox a look, one that only they understand.

"What did the two of you end up getting into last night?" Lachlan asks.

"You were with us," I answer.

"We were until Maggie started feeling sick. I took her back to her room and stayed with her to make sure she didn't need anything. We left the two of you at the casino. Mad was up ten grand when we left."

Maddox looks over at me and shrugs. "It's all a bit fuzzy," he confesses.

My mouth is still like cotton. I reach for the glass of water in front of me and hear a gasp.

"Aunt Brogan, you have a ring like Mommy. Did Forty give you a ring too?" Rayne asks.

I close my eyes, waiting for the floor to open up and swallow me. It's not until Maddox bails me out that I open them again to find everyone watching us.

"We got married last night," Maddox says as if his words are not life-changing.

The girls gasp, which makes Lilly do the same, mimicking them.

"You're married?" the twins ask at the same time.

"We are. That means, in the eyes of the law, I'm your uncle now."

River tilts her head to the side. "I thought you were already my uncle?"

"I was, but this just makes it official. Just like Forty when he married your mom. That makes it all official," Maddox tries to explain as I elbow him in the ribs. He turns to give me his full attention.

"What are you doing?"

"Explaining to our nieces."

"This is not real," I whisper hiss.

He leans close, his lips next to my ear, his words only for me. "Maybe it should be."

"Brogan?" Briar says my name, and there is so much she's saying with just her tone of voice.

Slowly, I turn to face my sister. "Briar."

Her eyes are shimmering with tears. "You're married." Her smile could light up Vegas.

"We were under the influence, and we're going to take care of it first thing tomorrow."

"Or not," Maddox says. This time, he doesn't lower his voice, and lets everyone at the table hear him.

"Maddox." I sigh. If he only knew what his words did to my heart. If he only knew that I've wanted him for so long, and knowing that he's mine, even temporarily, that I have to give him up, well, that's just pure torture. But I know how this ends. Maddox doesn't date. He's not a playboy, but I've never heard him say a single word about settling down. Unlike Forrest, who was all-in the day he laid eyes on my sister and my nieces.

His hand slides beneath the table and lands on my thigh. "We'll talk. Let's just enjoy breakfast."

I nod, because what else am I supposed to do? I'm married to the man I've wanted for months, and it kinda feels like he wants us to stay that way. We settle in for breakfast. I waver on the cinnamon rolls, and a fruit bowl, and decide to be good and get the bowl.

"I'll have the big breakfast platter, and add a cinnamon roll for my wife," Maddox tells our waiter.

I turn to look at him. "How did you know I was thinking about getting the cinnamon roll?" I ask him.

He leans in and presses his lips to my temple. "It's my job to know my wife." He flashes me a grin. "I saw you wavering, and I know you love them." He shrugs as if it's that simple.

"Maddox." I sigh again.

"We're enjoying breakfast. We'll talk when we get back to our room."

Our room.

We definitely need to talk. This isn't real. *We're* not real. I ignore the flutter in my chest. I don't deserve happily ever after. Not after what I let happen to my sister. I'm so happy she and the girls have found Forrest. She was always meant for great love. Me, on the other hand? I messed up, and I'll spend the rest of my life trying to make it up to her.

Maddox deserves better.

MADDOX 2

I CAN'T STOP TOUCHING HER.

My wife.

Fuck me, I love the sound of that. I don't remember much about last night. I do remember being thrilled to get time with her. I vaguely remember Maggie not feeling well and having a silent conversation with Lachlan, which is how he was the chosen one to take her back to the room.

After that, things get foggy. Really fucking foggy. But everything since the moment I woke up to realize my night ended in marrying Brogan is clear as a bright blue sky.

"Meet in the lobby in an hour?" Roman suggests. We've finished breakfast, and it's time to gather our things and head to the airport.

"We'll be there," I tell him. With a wave to our group, I place my hand on the small of Brogan's back and lead her toward the elevators. She's quiet as she stands next to me, watching as the numbers climb to our floor.

It's not until we're in our room, well, her room that became ours because she's now my wife, that she speaks.

"Maddox—" she starts, but when I reach for her, pulling her into my arms, she snaps her mouth shut. Those big green eyes stare up at me, and her hands rest on my chest.

"Yes, wife?" I ask with a tender smile. Damn, I thought Roman and Legend were crazy with all the "my wife" business they toss around. Forrest has joined them since Briar agreed to marry him. I didn't understand it, but now, I get it. I really fucking do. It's a rush like nothing I've ever felt before to know that this woman, this beautiful, smart, incredible woman is my wife.

Mine.

Damn, I love the sound of that.

"It's not real, Maddox." There is something in her tone of voice that tells me she's not exactly happy that her words are true. Well, it's real. She's my wife. Sure, we can't remember how it happened, and maybe that's what I'm hearing, but I'm going to choose to think she's sad when she says, "it's not real."

I raise my hand and wiggle my ring finger. "This and that paper sitting on the table say otherwise." I lift her left hand from my chest and kiss her white gold diamond band. I make a mental note to get her an engagement ring. Sure, we missed that step, but she still deserves one. "This too."

"We don't even remember it," she argues.

"So, we renew our vows." I'm already formulating a plan in my mind. It's genius really.

"Maddox. Can you be serious for five damn seconds so we can talk about this?" She huffs out an irritated breath.

Stepping away from her, I take her hand in mine and lead her to the bed. I sit and pull her onto my lap. I can't stop touching her, and I hope that it helps my cause, because now that she's mine in the eyes of the law, I want it to stay that way. I've wanted her for months and refused to do anything about it.

"I'm being serious," I assure her as I tuck a loose strand of hair behind her ear. She gives me a look that tells me she thinks I'm blowing smoke up her ass. I'm going to have to bare my soul to her.

I'm all-in and willing to fight for this. For her. For us. She's sitting sideways on my lap, but I need to look directly into her eyes for this. Lifting her from my lap, she squeaks in surprise as I set her back on the bed and drop to my knees. She automatically widens her legs, making room for me.

Resting my palms on her cheeks, I give her another tender smile. "Months. Since the first day I laid eyes on you, I've wanted you."

"W-What?" she whispers.

I nod. "At first, it was just that you were beautiful. You were this fun-loving aunt and sister, and as I got to know you, I knew you were someone I could see myself with."

"You never said anything."

"I didn't want you to know."

"Why?" She tilts her head to the side as she processes what I'm telling her.

"Because your sister and my best friend, my brother, are now married, and if this didn't work out, it would have been awkward."

"That's exactly why we need to make this go away."

I nod. "Yesterday, I would have agreed with you. Today, I'm seeing things differently."

"Explain that. I don't understand, Maddox."

"Today, I woke up with a wife. Not just any wife. It's you, Brogan. You're the one I want. I've wanted you quietly for months. Now that you're mine, I can't fathom changing that."

"Do you hear yourself? We weren't even dating, Maddox."

"Then we'll date," I say, shrugging.

"We're married! This isn't a game, Maddox." She pulls in a deep breath, trying to get a hold of her emotions. I watch as each one plays out in her features. Fear, confusion, and damn if I don't see hope shimmering in her eyes.

"I know, Brogan. I know that this isn't a game. I know that it's my life and yours. I know it sounds completely insane, but damn, baby, I don't want to end this. I want us to stay married. I want you to be mine." I pause, and since she doesn't reply, I keep going, spewing all the jumbled thoughts in my mind and in my heart, hoping to convince her this is what I want.

She is what I want.

I don't know what I can say to convince her. I just need time. Time to prove to her that we can be incredible. Time for her to fall in love with me. I've wanted her for so long. I need to give her time to catch up. I don't want to get a divorce. She's mine, and I want her to stay mine.

"Give me six months," I blurt.

Her brow furrows in confusion. "What?"

"Six months. Give me six months to prove to you that we are the real deal. We are endgame."

"You don't know that, Maddox. You don't even know me, not really. You might like the idea of a wife, but trust me, you don't want that person to be me."

"I do," I say firmly. It's not lost on me that those two words are what got us in this situation in the first place. "I know you, Brogan. I know that your nieces and your sister are your entire world. I know that you and your sister have been through hell and back and are still here fighting to tell your story. I know that I'm drawn to you like no one ever before, and I know that I want to give this a shot. Me and you."

"I'm broken, Maddox." She shakes her head, sorrow masking her features. "You don't want to take on all that is me right now. Trust me."

"Let me prove to you that I do. I want you. You're not broken, Brogan. You might be a little bruised, but you're stronger than your past."

"They told you." She nods, as if she wasn't sure if I knew her history.

"Emerson sat Lachlan and me down and told us what happened." Dropping my hands from her face, I stand and hug her tightly to my chest. It's not until I bend and rest my head on top of hers that I feel her arms wrap around me, returning my embrace. I hold her until she lets go, and even then, I hang on just a little longer before placing my index finger beneath her chin and tilting her eyes to mine.

"I'm a mess, Maddox," she says, tears shimmering in her eyes. "Therapy is helping, but I don't want to bring you down with all that."

"And what about Briar and Forrest? Is she bringing him down? Of course not. Those two are kindred spirits. How do you know that we're not?" I ask her.

"We're going to miss our flight," she says, changing the subject.

"Promise me we'll talk more about this when we get home?" She nods, but that's not good enough. "I need your words, Brogan."

"I promise we'll talk about this more when we get back to Tennessee."

I don't miss that she refused to say home, but that's okay. I've got the entire flight back to form a plan. Six months is all I need to prove to her that we're meant to be. Fate brought us together in that wedding chapel last night, and who are we to fight against fate?

"Are you packed?" she asks.

I glance over my shoulder to where my luggage sits. "Yeah, I just need to zip it all up. Do you need help?"

I'm greeted with a soft smile. "No. I can manage. Thank you, though."

"We make a great team, huh?" I say, winking at her.

She shakes her head, but she's unable to hide the corner of her mouth that's tilted up as she tries to fight her smile. "You're something else, Maddox Lanigan."

"Right back at you, Mrs. Lanigan." She sucks in a shocked breath, and I bite my cheek to keep from laughing. Instead, I lean in and kiss the corner of her mouth. "Go get packed, wife. We're going to miss our flight."

She opens her mouth to speak but snaps it closed, gives a slight shake of her head, and moves around me to start packing up her things. I take a trip around the room, making sure neither one of us left anything. That includes our marriage certificate. I store that safely in my carry-on suitcase. I make a mental note to frame it or maybe put it in a scrapbook or something when I get home. I'll have to ask Emerson what she suggests. She and Roman have been married the longest in our group.

Fifteen minutes later, I have both of our suitcases in hand as we roll into the lobby to meet everyone. We take the shuttle to the airport, and I make sure to sit next to her, keeping my hand on her thigh. On the flight home, she sits next to Maggie. I almost ask Maggie to switch with me but think better of it. She might need to talk to someone, although it's really quiet two rows up where they're sitting.

"So, you're a married man now, huh?" Lachlan asks.

"Yep."

"How long do you think it will take to get it annulled?"

"We're not getting an annulment." I turn to glare at my best friend to find him grinning like a fool.

"I'm just fucking with you. I heard you loud and clear at breakfast this morning. You really want to stay married?"

"To Brogan? Yes." Lachlan doesn't mask the shock on his face. I exhale and rest my head back against the seat. "I've had a thing for her for a while now."

"Yeah, I got that, but married? You're not even dating."

"Because I was too damn worried about fucking it up to make a move. Drunk me had more balls than sober me, and this is my chance, Lach."

"So, did she agree?"

"Not yet, but she will."

"What can I do?"

"Nothing. This is all on me. I have to show her that being married to me is what she wants."

"Is it? I mean, do you think that's what she wants?"

"I think that she's scared. I think that their past has made her feel as though she's not worthy, and fuck me, but I want to be the man to show her that she is."

"I'll talk you up," he says, no humor at all in his tone.

Opening my eyes, I turn to look at him to find him nodding and wearing a serious expression. "Thanks, man, but this is on me. I have to figure out how to make my wife fall in love with me."

"Do you love her?"

"I care about her. A lot. Enough that I want to see what we can be."

"And if it doesn't work out?" he asks.

I glare at him, and he laughs. "It will."

"You're sunk, my friend." Reaching over, he taps my chest. "You might want to look a little deeper."

"Fuck off," I grumble. I can't say that I'm in love with her, but I do know I care about her, and yeah, I could see myself falling fast and hard for my wife. I just need her to give us a chance. I've always followed my gut instinct and my gut is telling me she's the one. That we can do this and be happy. We can build a life together.

Lachlan and I both sleep the remainder of the flight. When we land, I rush to grab my bag, and I'm out of my seat to help Brogan and Maggie before the aisle can get blocked and she sneaks away from me.

"My place or yours?" I ask her once we're off the plane.

"What?"

"Are we staying at my place or yours tonight?"

"Maddox." She sighs, and I get the feeling she's going to be sighing my name a lot.

"You promised me we would talk," I remind her.

"My place."

"Okay." I nod and continue to carry her bag and mine to the parking garage. When I don't stop at Legend's SUV and keep going to my truck, she calls my name.

"Maddox."

I stop and turn to look at her. "Yes, dear?" I smirk.

"I rode with Legend and Monroe."

"I know you did, but we're going home, baby. You can ride with me." I watch as acceptance washes over her face. She turns toward Briar and gives her a hug, before doing the same with Forrest. I'm too far away to hear what they're saying, but close enough to know it's about me.

Then she kneels and tugs River and Rayne into a hug. The girls giggle before they wiggle out of her hold and take off, racing toward me. I have just enough time to drop the bags and crouch down to catch them.

"Bye, Uncle Maddox."

Uncle Maddox.

Damn.

They've called me that hundreds of times, but this time, it rings more true than ever, and I'm not too insecure to admit that it gets me in the chest. My heart squeezes. These little angels have stolen all of our hearts.

"Bye, girls. Be good for your mom and dad."

I glance up at Forrest, and he's smiling wide. "Come on, girls. Daddy will strap you in your seats." His eyes find mine, and he mouths, "I'm a daddy." It's still hard for him to wrap his head around the changes in his life most days, but it's because he loves those three so damn much.

One more hug for me, and they're off racing toward their dad. I stand, and Forrest gives me a nod and a silent confirmation that he's with me on this. He understands the Pearce women. He's married to one, too, and he knows what I'm up against. His look says, "Stay strong. I'm with you, and don't give up on what you want."

What I want is Brogan.

I want my wife.

I want the chance to make her fall in love with me.

I remain where I am while Brogan slowly makes her way over to me. I pick up our bags and we walk side by side to my truck. I open the back door and place our luggage inside before opening her door for her.

"You don't have to open doors for me."

"I know I don't have to, but I want to." What I don't tell her is that she deserves to be treated like a queen. My queen.

The drive to her place is quiet, but not uncomfortable. I want to reach over and take her hand in mine, but I refrain. I know I'm coming on strong, but I'm not the kind of man who sits back and waits. I did that once in my life. With her. It was hell seeing her and not pursuing her. It's my second chance to have her in my life as more than just a friend, or my best friend's sister-in-law, and that's worth fighting for.

I let fear hold me back, and that was a mistake, one I'm currently paying for because my feelings for her are like a bomb in her eyes. She didn't expect them. I just hope she agrees to give me a chance to show her what we can be.

Who we can be together.

BROGAN 3

MADDOX PULLS HIS TRUCK INTO my driveway and puts it in Park. The house is dark, and loneliness washes over me. I've been living here on my own for a while, but tonight it feels different. The emptiness that waits for me is pressing into my chest like a ton of bricks.

"I'll get your door," he says, his voice gruff from the silence on the drive home from the airport.

I clear my throat. "I can get it."

Maddox reaches over and places his hand on my arm. "Let me, Brogan." There's an earnest look in his eyes, almost pleading. I give him a subtle nod. We need to talk anyway.

A few seconds later, he's pulling open the passenger door and offering me his hand. "Let's get you inside," he says.

I take his hand and climb out of the truck. The winter air whips around us. Maddox places his hand on the small of my back and starts to lead me toward the house. "My bag."

"I'll come back and get it. Let's get you inside where it's warm."

I want to argue with him. I want to tell him I'm not fragile, but suddenly, I feel fragile. As if I'm a piece of glass that can shatter in an instant. I'm happy for my sister and my nieces. They're living their happily ever after, one I'm certain Forrest will work tirelessly to provide for them.

However, as my husband guides me up onto the front porch of my empty home, that's all I feel.

Empty.

Lonely.

I've been doing this on my own for several weeks now. This isn't new, but it feels new. The weight of the drunken mistake Maddox and I made, coupled with the fact that it's finally sinking in that my sister and my nieces aren't coming home, presses heavily against my chest. They're not just having an extended stay at Forrest's house. He's their family now. They're his, and I'm just me.

I'm jolted out of my thoughts when Maddox bends over and lifts me into his arms. I yelp in surprise and wrap my arms around his neck to hold on tight. "What are you doing? Put me down," I scold. I swear this man has lost his grip on reality.

"Can't do that. As your husband, it's my duty to carry you over the threshold."

"Maddox." I sigh. Partly because I'm exhausted already and we haven't really discussed how we are going to handle this. Not in depth. And the other part? That part melts for this man. I've wanted him for so long, and it cracks my heart wide open, knowing he deserves better than someone who is broken and can't trust. If only things were different. If only my past didn't control so much of my present. I've been working with my therapist, the one that Briar and I are both seeing. I'm better, but I'm still... not good enough for a man like Maddox.

Maddox Lanigan is covered in tattoos, his muscles have muscles, and his smile... it melts me every single time he flashes it my way. He's everything every woman wants, well, everything I want, but I know what I bring to the table. Anxiety, trust issues, and fear. Fear of losing those I love. That's all I really know, losing people. Sure, I have my sister and her twin daughters, but I've lost them, too, in a way. We were a team, the four of us, and now they have a new team they're playing for, and that's okay. I'm happy for them, but I'm really fucking sad for me.

Everyone I love leaves in one way or another, and I know I wouldn't be able to handle losing Maddox if I allowed myself to think of him as mine.

"Type in the code, baby."

I want to argue, but instead, I type in the passcode for the front door and twist the handle. Maddox kicks it gently with his foot and steps inside with me in his arms. He carries us toward the couch, and instead of placing me back on my feet, he turns and sits, leaving me on his lap. I try to scramble free, but his hold is too tight.

"Let me hold you," he mumbles, and I immediately stop trying to move off his lap. "Thank you." He pushes my hair behind my ear.

"Thank you for the ride."

He smirks. "You're welcome. That's the least I can do for my new bride."

I release a heavy sigh. "Come on, Maddox. Let's be real. We have to get this marriage annulled."

"We don't have to." He gives me a pleading puppy-dog look.

"We do. We're not in love, Maddox. We went to Vegas, drank too much, and got married in our drunken stupor. That is not the makings of a successful marriage."

"Think of the story we'll tell our kids and grandkids."

My heart squeezes inside my chest. "No kids. No grandkids."

"Really?" he asks, surprised. "You don't want kids?"

"I want kids. *We're* not having kids. We're not married, Maddox. Not really. We're not even dating."

"Then date me. While we're married," he adds quickly.

"What?" I still can't believe this is his response to the situation we've found ourselves in.

"I care about you," he says. His voice is soft, and the look in his eyes tells me he believes what he's saying, too bad I can't allow myself to believe him. "Like I said. For months, I've wanted you, but thought I had to stay away. I didn't want to complicate things with Forrest and Briar. What if we didn't work out? Where would that leave our group? I pushed what I wanted to the back burner, and I regret it. Maybe we could have had a double wedding." He winks.

I want to tell him that I've felt the same way, but I can't find the words. My heart is currently celebrating that this amazing man wants me. Wants me, even if we can't stay married. My heart is racing like I just ran a 5K.

"It's still too complicated. My sister is still married to your best friend. Our lives are still too intertwined."

"But what if it isn't too complicated?" Maddox asks. "What if it's everything we could have ever imagined for ourselves?"

"But what if it isn't?" I counter. At this point, we both sound like broken records, and we keep talking in circles.

"Brogan, you feel it, right? This spark that ignites between us?"

It's on the tip of my tongue to lie to him, but that's not who I am. "Yeah," I agree softly. "But, Maddox, sparks don't mean we should stay married."

"I get it. It's not ideal, but, Brogan, I've wanted you for a long damn time, and now that you're mine, I can't let you go."

"You have to." I stand from his lap, and this time, he lets me. "I need to use the restroom." Okay, so that's a lie, but not completely. I do need to use the restroom as a place of reprieve and to put some distance between us. His scent and his arms wrapped around me is altering my ability to think clearly.

"I'll be here." He smiles softly, and damn him, my heart melts. He's such a great guy—kind, and caring, and sexy as hell. In another life, I would jump at the chance to be married to him, but it just won't work. It's too complicated. There are too many wires in our lives that are crossed. His best friend, my sister, my nieces. He's thinking the glass is half full, and I'm a half-empty girl. Life experience has taught me hope is fickle at best.

Once inside the bathroom, I twist the lock and brace my hands on the counter. Bowing my head, I focus on pulling in a deep breath. How did I let this happen? I never drink too much. I never let myself indulge like that. Not after what happened the summer after high school graduation. That's not me, and it's freaking me out that I don't remember.

My cell rings, breaking me out of my thoughts. I rush to pull it out of my back pocket to see Briar's name on the screen. "Hey you," I answer, trying to hide the anxiety that's coursing through my veins.

"Did you make it home okay?" she asks.

"I did. Maddox drove me home." He's still sitting in my living room.

"Husbands are good for that," she teases.

I groan. "Not you too."

My sister laughs. "I couldn't help myself."

"How did I let this happen, Briar? I don't let myself get out of control, not after—" I stop because if anyone knows why I keep a tight leash on my drinking and actions, it's my sister.

"You don't see it, do you?"

"I guess not. Enlighten me, ole wise one."

"You feel safe with him, Brogan. Last night you knew that no matter what, Maddox would take care of you."

"He was drunk too!" I say a little too loudly and peer at the door, waiting for Maddox to knock.

"He was, but you knew even then he would never hurt you." She stops there, giving her words a chance to sink in. "He's a good man, Brogan. He cares about you."

"We're friends."

"Friends don't look at each other the way Maddox looks at you. Don't think I haven't noticed how you look at him, too, when you think no one is watching."

"Whatever," I grumble. She's right, at least about me watching him. I can't seem to help myself. The man is perfection, but that's still not reason enough to stay married. "He wants to stay married."

"You like him. I'll even go as far as to say that you care about him."

"We're not even dating. We can't just wake up married after a drunken night in Vegas and say, 'Hey, let's give this a whirl.' That's insane, Briar."

"Meh," she replies. "If I've learned anything since meeting Forrest, it's that this is our life. We only get one and we can do with it what we choose. Living in fear keeps you from experiencing some of the most blissful moments."

"We know that life isn't all sunshine and rainbows," I remind her.

"We do. That's why we fight harder for the good times. It took me time, but I let Forrest in, and now look at us. The girls and I have our happily ever after."

"You dated first," I mumble.

"Who cares? Toss society's rules out of the window. This is your life, Brogan. You get to decide what makes you happy."

"What happens when it doesn't work out?"

"*If.* *If* it doesn't work out, and you don't know how it's going to end. None of us do. All you can do is give it everything you have and see where it takes you."

Her words give me hope. "Now you sound like Susan," I tell her. Susan is the therapist that we both started seeing a couple of months ago. She's incredible and talking to her on my own and with my sister has helped me so much to get over the traumas of our past, but I'm still a work in progress.

"So I sound intelligent? Thanks, sis," she teases.

"I should get back out there."

"Out where?"

"The living room. I needed a few minutes, so I locked myself in the bathroom," I admit. "Maddox is waiting for me." I don't say might be, because I know him well enough to understand he's not going anywhere until we make a decision that could affect our entire group of friends and family, not just us.

"You can trust him, Brogan. Take a gamble; you might be surprised where that chance leads you. I love you, big sister." I can hear the smile in her voice. As twins, I'm two minutes older and she very rarely admits to me being her big sister.

"Love you too." I end the call, shove my phone back into my jeans pocket, exhale, and twist the lock before pulling open the door.

"Everything okay?" Maddox asks as soon as he sees me.

"Yeah. Sorry, Briar called. She just wanted to make sure I made it home okay."

He nods and pats the couch cushion next to him. Once I've taken my seat, he turns to face me, and I do the same. Our knees are touching, and I ignore the heat that flows from his body to mine.

"I'm a simple man, Brogan. I love my friends and the business we've built with our blood, sweat, and tears. I love my family. I pay my taxes, I don't lie or cheat, and I keep my promises."

These are all things I knew about him already. Well, maybe not the taxes part, but one can only assume being one fifth of a successful growing business, paying taxes is a given. Why he's telling me all this is yet to be determined. I open my mouth to ask, but he takes my hand in his, and I clamp my mouth shut.

"I've always followed my gut. Once in my life, I didn't, and this—me and you—that's fate's way of telling me I fucked up and is fixing my mistake. I want you, Brogan. I want to come home to you. I want to cuddle with you on the couch after a long day at the shop. I want to hold you as you drift off to sleep, and I want to be the first person you see each morning when you wake up."

"Maddox...." My voice trails off because what do I say to that?

"I know we aren't dating, but we should have been. I should have followed my gut. My instincts were telling me you were the one. That's my fuck up, and I won't make it twice, which is why I have a proposition for you."

"What kind of proposition?"

Maddox stands from his seat on the couch, only to kneel again. I turn my body to face him, and he takes my hands in his. "Give me six months. To date you. To show you how good we will be together. Give me six months to make you fall in love with me."

"So, you want to date, but only for six months?"

"Yes, well no. I want to date you, but not as my girlfriend. As my wife. I want to date my wife." He gives me an adorable, endearing grin that's hard as hell to resist. "I want us to give this everything we have."

"I already care about you. Six months with you, to let you go. That's going to bring heartbreak and confusion, and a whole lot of messiness with our friends and family."

"Baby, you have us divorced before we even try. Trust me, I know for certain if you kick my ass to the curb after six months, my heart will be in tattered pieces all over the living room floor. You're worth the risk. I believe in what we could be." He lifts my hand and places it over his heart. "You and me, Mrs. Lanigan. Six months."

"What happens if in that time we're still not sure?" I don't need that long. I know my heart will be pulverized if I have him for any amount of time, only for him to walk away. But I've lived through worse. That's the story of my life. That's the way my book was written.

"I'm pretty sure that's enough time to know if we're falling harder than what we already are."

"What does that look like? Us dating?"

"Married and dating. We live together. My place or yours, but you have more space. We sleep next to one another and share our lives with each other. I want you twisted in every fiber of my life, and my soul, Brogan."

I want that. I want it all. Everything he just said, I want more than anything, but I don't deserve it. Maybe I should just take what time I can get with him, and when he realizes I'm a mess of epic proportions, he'll cut ties, and I can quietly lick my wounds.

"I don't trust easily. I'll drive you insane with all of my questions and the constant need for reassurance. I'm broken, Maddox. I'm working on it, but it's a long road to travel."

"Let me take that road with you." His eyes are locked on mine. "Let me be the man who stands next to you and gives you all the reassurance you need. Ask me as many questions as you want. I'll answer every single one of them with nothing but complete honesty."

"Don't say I didn't warn you," I tell him.

A slow, sexy smile tugs at his lips. "I need to hear you say it, baby."

"Six months." I nod, letting him know that I'm agreeing. My heart tells me this is a grand plan, while my head is full of the opposite. However, it's my heart that's leading this time, and the way it's racing at the thought of Maddox being mine, even for a short amount of time, sets something ablaze inside me. Something a lot like hope infused with happiness.

"Six months what?"

"We date for six months." I can't believe I'm agreeing to this. It's crazy, and not me at all, but it's not like he's a stranger. I know Maddox; at least I'm pretty sure I do. Anxiety starts to kick in, but he rests his palms on my cheeks, bringing me out of my thoughts.

"Focus on me, baby."

I nod again. "We stay married. Six months. Dating."

He smirks. "We have one more decision to make."

"What's that?"

"Your place or mine?"

"I love this house. It was my grandmother's."

"Can I tell you a secret?" His hands are still cupping my face. His eyes, still laser focused on mine.

"Yes," I whisper, like there are other people here to listen to our conversation.

"I love this house. I kept waiting for it to go on the market, but it never did. I saw that someone had moved in. I never could have imagined it would have been my future wife."

"Stop." I laugh.

"I'm telling you the truth. Ask the guys. I even told them when we were here for the first time for the girls' birthday party back in the summer."

"Well, I guess that means you're my new roommate."

"Husband, roommate, bedmate, secret keeper, question answerer, and whatever else you want me to be. I want you to be mine, Brogan. My everything."

His answer is honest, and playful, and it feels normal for us, and what we've been to one another up to this point. "Does that mean you're mine?" I hate that I ask the question, and I bite down on my bottom lip, pissed at myself for letting the question fall from my lips.

His eyes soften. "That's exactly what it means." He removes his left hand from my face and wiggles his fingers, his wedding band on full display. "Only you, Brogan."

"Gah, are we really doing this?" I ask. I feel giddy at the thought, and if I'm being honest, I can't believe I'm agreeing to this.

"You already agreed. No take backs. Besides, you said 'I do'."

"Do you remember it? The wedding?"

He shakes his head. "No, but I wish I did. We'll have to plan another one so we can remember it."

"Six months," I remind him.

"I don't need six days. I want this. I want you. I've been falling hard for you for the last several months. These feelings are not new for me. I understand it's going to take you some time to catch up. Just know that mine are only going to grow."

"Do we hide this? That we got drunk married?"

"No. Fuck that. No. I'm not hiding. We're married. You are my wife. We're in this all the way, Brogan. Sure, it's unconventional, but our life is what we make it, and I want to make it with you."

"Charmer."

"Only for my wife." He leans forward and presses his lips to the corner of my mouth. "Let me run outside and grab our bags. I only have one client tomorrow, so I'll bring over more of my stuff then."

"Okay."

He climbs to his feet, presses his lips to the top of my head, and goes out to grab our bags. I remain where I'm sitting on the couch and let my new reality sink in.

I'm married.

I'm married to Maddox.

My life is about to get turned upside down. That's what hope does to you. Then again, maybe it's my nervous excitement at the mere thought of it being just the two of us, even for a short amount of time. I can admit that I want to be wrong. I want to be his, and I want him to be mine more than anything.

I guess only time will tell.

MADDOX 4

THE WINTER WIND SLAPS ME across the face as I reach inside the back seat of my truck for our bags. It doesn't matter because I'm going back into the warm house to sleep in a warm bed beside my wife.

My wife.

When I boarded the plane to Vegas, I was hopeful that I'd get to spend some time with her. I was going to volunteer to take the twins, and I knew she would help me, but Roman and Emerson beat me to it. It made sense considering they had Lilly, and those three, even with the age difference, are thick as thieves.

My plan failed, but it turned out better than I could have hoped for. The four of us taking in Vegas, and when Maggie started to feel ill, and Lachlan offered to go back to the hotel with her, I knew there was some higher power cheering me on. What I didn't know is that we'd wake up married, but I have no regrets.

Well, maybe one. I would have liked to remember the moment that I stared into her eyes and promised to love, honor, and cherish her for all time. I know it was a Vegas wedding, but surely, the sentiment was the same.

I know I would have said the words and meant them. I didn't tell Brogan that I loved her, because I didn't want to scare her away. There is also a part of me that's not really sure that's what I'm feeling. I've never been in love before. However, I know that I think about her all the time. I always try to sit next to her, beg for a spot on her blanket like I did back on the Fourth of July. I crave being next to her, and she is, in fact, the most beautiful woman I've ever laid eyes on.

Is that love? I think so. My wife has agreed to give us six months for both of us to find out. After slamming the truck door, I jog back to the house and the warmth of its four walls. Brogan is still sitting on the couch, but stands and rushes toward me when I step inside and shut the door.

"I got it, babe," I tell her when she reaches for her bag. "I'll just put these in the bedroom." I pause. "Is that okay with you? If I sleep next to you?" I want to not give her the option, but I know her past and how her choices were taken from her, and I never want to be that man. No matter how much I crave falling asleep next to her.

She nods and steps back, allowing me to walk past her. I know where her bedroom is. I helped Forrest move Briar and the girls in with him, so I make my way down the hallway to the last door on the right, and step inside.

I'm immediately assaulted by the smell of honeysuckle. I know it's her body lotion because I flat out asked her a few months ago. The smell wraps around me like a warm embrace. I don't think it's really hit me that this is where I'll be sleeping for the next six months. With her wrapped in my arms, surrounded by honeysuckle in the dead of winter.

How is this my life?

How did I manage to marry the girl of my dreams and convince her to give us a shot?

I know how lucky I am, and I plan to show her every single day what being mine feels like. It's funny because the reality is that I'm hers too. There isn't anything I wouldn't do for her. "Being mine," that's just words. She's the one who holds the power in this marriage, and if I'm being honest, I wouldn't want it any other way. This is Brogan's world, and I'm just living in it.

Now, to convince her that the two of us, as Mr. and Mrs. living in her world, is where we were both meant to be.

Once I've placed our bags at the foot of the bed, I head back out to the living room. I don't see Brogan, so I move to the kitchen to find her pouring a glass of milk.

"Want one?" she asks.

"Sure." I move to the island and take a seat as she pushes a second tall glass of milk my way.

"When do you go back to work?" We all took some time off for the wedding and since it's also New Year's, I'm not sure what her schedule looks like.

"I took an extra day. I figured I'd be tired from all the travel, so I don't go back until the third. What about you?"

"I have one client tomorrow afternoon, as far as I know." I pull out my phone, log into the app for our scheduling system, and look at my schedule. "That's it. I'm going to go ahead and block out the rest of my day so I can move some of my stuff."

"Can you do that? Just block out your day?"

"Yeah, we all maintain our own schedules. Looks like all four of the guys are on the books tomorrow. They won't miss me."

"The five of you have really built something special."

Pride swells in my chest at her acknowledgment of what my four best friends and I have built. "Thank you. It's surreal to see the business grow like it has. Who would have thought we'd be this successful with our art? Because tattooing was not something they talked about on career day." I chuckle.

Brogan smiles. "Right? There are so many trades that are never discussed. Working hard and chasing your dreams. The five of you are proof that if you do that, you can have success."

"What about you? Did you always want to be a phlebotomist?" I feel like I should already know the answer to this question, but I've never asked. I'm going to make it a point to learn every tiny detail about my wife.

"Honestly, I wanted to be a nurse. After everything that happened, there wasn't time or money for nursing school. It was a way for me to have a career that didn't take years of schooling, and still be in the medical field."

"There's still time you know. You can go back to school and get your nursing degree."

She smiles, but it's not one of happiness. Her eyes show her sadness. "Who's going to keep the lights on in this place if I do that?" she asks.

"Me."

Her body stiffens as she studies me, holding my stare. "Nursing school is longer than six months, Maddox."

"Good thing I don't plan on leaving in six months," I counter.

"I'm too old to go back now."

"Brogan, babe, you're twenty-three. That's not too old. Hell, you could be fifty-three, and I'd still tell you to go for it if that's what you wanted."

"I'm a different person now. Too much time has passed. Too much has happened."

"Think about it." I can tell she's not going to, but if this is something she truly wants, I'm going to make sure she gets it.

"What about you? How did the five of you come to open Everlasting Ink?" she asks, changing the subject, and I let her.

"Honestly, we've all been friends since we were kids, and all five of us loved art. When we graduated, we all went to get tattoos and it just sort of clicked. That's what we wanted to do. Since then, we worked our asses off to build a name for our business, and thanks to Legend's help, we're opening a new state-of-the-art facility here in Ashby."

"I've heard bits and pieces. Something about an inheritance?"

"Yeah, his grandma that he never met. There was a stipulation that he had to be married for a year to anyone of his choosing to get the money. He wasn't going to go through with it until Monroe volunteered."

"And they lived happily ever after," she murmurs.

"Pretty much. We could all see it from day one. There was nothing fake about their marriage."

"Not like ours," she replies.

"Baby, there is nothing fake about our marriage either."

"We don't even remember it. Besides, all we have is a piece of paper that says we had a wedding. It's just paperwork at this point."

I shrug. "Then we'll renew our vows. We'll give ourselves a day we can remember." The idea was already brewing in my mind. All she has to do is agree, and I'll make it happen. Whatever she wants, it's hers.

"I never drink that much. Never. Not after... that night." She seems to close in on herself as her shoulders hunch together. "It was stupid of me to allow myself to get in that state. It was dangerous."

"I was with you. I'd never let anything happen to you."

"You were wasted too. You can't remember that night either, so really, you can't say that you would have protected me."

My eyes stay locked on hers. "I can promise you, Brogan, that even wasted, I'd protect you."

"You can't know that. I've been there, Maddox. I've woken in a room I don't recognize after a night of drinking. What's worse is that I only had one drink that night. I was young and dumb, and didn't even consider those frat guys would slip something into our drinks. My sister—" Her voice cracks. "She wasn't as lucky as me. I'm the older sister. It was my job to protect her."

"You're twins." I feel stupid saying that since obviously she knows, but she's struggling with her past, fighting against guilt that's not hers to fight. They're both innocent in this. I don't know how to make her see that, but I'm going to find a way.

"I'm two minutes older, Maddox. It was my job."

I don't know what to say to her. Nothing I say will reach her. Not tonight. She needs to see my actions speak for me. She needs to know that I'm here, and I'm not going anywhere, but I have to prove that to her. I'm surprised she's opened up to me like she has, but I know why. She's thinking if she's honest about her past, it will push me away.

She's wrong.

Hearing that night from her point of view only makes me want to hold on to her a little tighter. I want to wrap her in my arms and protect her from everything. I want to shower her with my love, support, and understanding until she doesn't know where she ends and I begin.

Her eyes well with tears, and that's more than I can handle. I can't take it. Standing, I go to her side of the kitchen island. I move in behind her and wrap my arms around her, burying my face in her neck. Her back is pressed to my front, and I feel her inhale a heavy breath before slowly exhaling.

"What are you doing?" she whispers.

"Holding you. You looked like you needed a hug, and that's my job, Brogan. As your husband, I'm here for you. I needed you to know that." She doesn't try to move, but she does relax into my arms.

I don't know how long we stand here, but eventually, I release her and step back. She grabs her milk, downs it, and steps around me to rinse her cup before placing it in the sink.

"You ready for bed?"

"We're really doing this?"

"We are."

"Yeah." She releases a shaky breath. "I'm ready for bed."

I hold my hand out to her, and she stares at it for a few seconds before she places hers in mine. Together, we move around the house, locking the front door and shutting off all the lights before I guide her down the hall to our room.

Our room.

"What side of the bed do you want?" she asks.

"I'll take the one closest to the door." She doesn't ask me why, and I don't tell her. She simply moves to grab clothes to change into and disappears into the bathroom. I take the opportunity to strip down to my boxer briefs and climb under the covers.

When Brogan opens the door, the light from the bathroom spills into the dark bedroom, and she stops, staring right at me. "Everything okay?"

"Yep." She turns off the light and makes her way to the opposite side of the bed in the dark room.

The bed dips when she climbs under the covers, and I smile when I see her lying on the edge. That's not going to work for me. Turning to my side, I whisper her name. "Brogan." I wait for her reply. I can hear her breathing, but eventually, she answers.

"Yeah?"

"Why are you not in my arms?" My question lingers between us.

"I don't know how to do this, Maddox. I've never... slept in the same bed with a man. Not any time that I can remember."

The truth of her words hit me like a kick to the gut. Our wedding night is bringing up terrible memories for her, and I hate that. I hate that I can't take that night all those years ago away from her.

"I'm not just any man, Brogan. I'm your husband. I'm your friend." I'm hoping that reminding her will ease some of her fears. "I'd never hurt you. Never."

"What do I do?" Her voice is soft, and she sounds broken, and it's killing me.

"You slide over here and let me wrap my arms around you. Then you use my chest as your pillow and you sleep soundly, knowing that I'm here. I'm here, and I'm not going anywhere. You're not alone, Brogan. Not now, not ever again." It's a vow that I intend to keep.

"Won't I be in your way?"

"Never. In fact, I don't think I can sleep knowing you're right beside me, and I'm not holding you. You can trust me. I just want to hold you." I wait for her reply that doesn't come. Instead, she lifts the blanket and slides closer, and I move to meet her in the middle of the bed. I open my arms wide and she settles next to me. My arms wrap around her, holding her close. Just when I'm about to let go, I feel the first drops of her tears against my bare chest. I don't know what to do. I hate her tears, but something tells me that they've been a long time coming. Forrest had a massive wall to scale with Briar. I'll climb to the very top to help Brogan knock down every single fear she might have.

I want to tell her not to cry, that I'll tackle all of her demons, but I don't. Instead, I place my lips on top of her head and hold her tighter.

"I've got you," I whisper. "I'm here." I rub her back gently while keeping one arm locked around her, and eventually, her tears stop, and her breathing evens out. I stare up at the ceiling with my heart cracked wide open.

I'm going to help her.

Regardless of whether she falls in love with me, I'm going to help her. I want to be her light in the darkness, and I want to be the solid foundation she can lean on. She's been fighting in silence. I'm sure, thinking her sister had it worse than she did. And instead of taking the time to heal, she's pushed her pain to the back and focused on helping Briar raise the girls.

This pain in my chest, the ache that seeing her in pain causes me, can only be one thing. I wasn't certain, but in just a few hours' time, I see clearly.

"I'm falling hard for you," I whisper to the dark room and my slumbering wife.

BROGAN 5

MY EYES SNAP OPEN AS I take stock of my current situation. I'm in my room, in my bed, with Maddox wrapped around me.

Maddox Lanigan is in my bed.

I give myself a few seconds to let the reason why sink in. I let yesterday's conversation float through my mind. I agreed to give him six months. Selfishly, I said yes, because for me, I want to know what it's like to be his, even just for a little while. I know my heart will be crushed when he leaves, but that's okay. What is it they say? It's better to have loved and lived than to never have loved at all? Or something close to that. I'm not in love with Maddox, but I do care about him, and the attraction is there. Which is why I need to get out of this bed.

Slowly, I lift his arm, but he grumbles and holds me tighter. I count to ten in my head, and try again.

"Too early," he mumbles.

"I have to pee." It's not a lie. It's also not the only reason I need out of this bed. I know myself well enough to understand that I crave time with him. Watching him from afar all these months, pretending to be aloof to his charms, I won't be able to do that if he's touching me.

"Come back to me," he mumbles.

"Uh-huh." I'd agree to just about anything if he lets me up. I feel his lips press against my shoulder before he relinquishes his hold on me, and I scramble out from underneath the covers and into the bathroom, making sure to twist the lock. I take care of business, wash my hands, and brush my teeth, all at a snail's pace. It's my hope that Maddox has fallen back asleep and I can slip out of the room without him noticing.

Finally, when I realize I've been in here far too long, I flip off the light, twist the lock, and open the door. I tiptoe over the threshold, trying not to make a sound. I'm two steps from the bedroom door when I hear his voice.

"You were supposed to come back to me."

I stop and inhale a deep breath before turning to face him. I swallow hard as I take him in. He's sitting up in bed with his back against the headboard and his abs on display. His eyes are sleepy, and there's a red mark on his cheek from how he was lying.

"I didn't want to wake you."

He pats the bed next to him. "I'm awake. Come back to bed. It's early."

"I'm used to getting up early. Not much time for sleeping in with four-year-old twins running around."

"Well, they're not here today. Come back to bed, Brogan."

I waver, unsure what to do. I want more than anything to slide in next to him and snuggle into his chest, but I shouldn't. "Go back to sleep," I tell him. "I'm going to make some coffee."

Maddox tosses the covers off him and climbs out of bed. My eyes fall to his boxer briefs and the very notable erection. I quickly look away. He stops next to me and presses his lips to my forehead.

"I woke up with my wife in my arms. It's not something I can control. Not that I want to." Another quick peck in the same spot on my forehead, and he steps back and toward the bathroom.

"I'll meet you in the kitchen." He strides into the bathroom, not bothering to shut the door. I hear him start to pee, and heat coats my cheeks.

I rush out of the room and down the hall to the kitchen. This was a bad idea. A very bad idea. I don't have experience with men. None. Nothing but some over-the-clothes groping during my senior year of college. After that night at the frat party, I steered clear, and then it was all about helping my sister and my dad. Since then, I've been helping raise the girls. I told myself I didn't have time, but it was more than that. My therapist helped me realize that.

I'm scared.

I have very few memories of the night that changed our lives, and I hate that. I hate being out of control, and men, well, they intimidate me. Not in the sense that I'm afraid of all men, but intimacy. Hell yes. I'm a twenty-three-year-old virgin, and as far as I can remember, I've never seen—outside of porn—a penis that I can remember.

So, yeah, seeing my husband, who I married while drunk in Vegas, hard after waking up next to me caused my cheeks to blush. I'm in over my head here. I never should have said yes to him.

I try to calm my heated libido. I put all of my attention on the coffeepot, which is why I didn't hear Maddox come into the kitchen. In fact, it's not until I feel his hands on my hips and his lips brushing against my neck, with his mumbled, "Morning, baby," that I even know he's here with me.

"Morning," I reply, because ignoring him doesn't feel right. "What time is your client?" I ask, remembering he has one this afternoon sometime.

"Not until two. It's a new client, and the note says, *uncertain*. This could be a long appointment or a short one." He chuckles.

"Does that happen often?"

"Not a lot, but you'd be surprised by the people who come in for an appointment with no idea what they want on their body for the rest of their lives."

"That's a big decision." I nod. "You don't seem to have that same issue." I let my eyes trail over his body. Did I mention he's still only in his boxer briefs? When I reach his face, he's smirking, and I quickly avert my gaze to the coffeepot as I watch it brew.

"Wasn't an issue for me. Do you have any tattoos?"

"No. Briar and I said we were going to get them growing up, but once we were old enough and didn't need our dad's permission, life threw us for a tailspin, and we never did."

"Well, when you're ready, I hear your husband is pretty damn good at what he does." He smirks.

I can't help but laugh. "I'll keep that in mind." The coffeepot splutters, letting me know it's done, and I get busy making our coffees. I've spent enough time with Maddox to know he likes his black, whereas I take two sugars and two creams in mine. I slide Maddox his cup as I take a quick pull of mine, only it comes off more like a slurp. Apparently, embarrassing myself in front of my new husband is the only thing I'm capable of doing these days.

"Thank you." He smiles and doesn't seem to mind I'm slurping my coffee like an addict jonesing for her next fix. "I'm going to shower and then run to my place to grab some more clothes and my laptop, and whatever else I can find that I think I might need. I'll pack the rest later and get the guys to help me move it all. I'll probably just put my furniture in storage."

"That seems like a lot of hassle for six months."

"You agreed to six months, but, Brogan, we're endgame, baby. You can come over to my place and see if there is anything of mine furniture wise you want to use here," he says, as if selling his furniture or putting it into storage is no big issue. "We can figure out what to do with it later. Now, I just want to be here with you. I'm giving you and this marriage everything I have, Brogan."

I swallow a burning gulp of coffee, letting his words sink in. "We agreed to this. For the time being, this is your home," I say. Do I think it's a waste of time for him to put everything in storage for six months? Sure, but he's a grown man and can decide for himself. Who am I to tell him what to do? I tried to tell him I was a mess, and he still insists we can do this whole being drunk-married thing and find our happily ever after. "Bring whatever you need or want to make this place feel like home."

"You, Brogan. You make this place my home."

"I don't know what to say to that."

"Say what you feel. I want this to work between us. Communication is an important part of every marriage and every relationship. It's just me, Brogan. You can tell me anything. You can say anything. I'm still going to be here."

"This is a lot, Maddox. We went from acquaintances, friends of friends if you will, to being married, and you're talking like we're forever."

"We were friends. More than acquaintances. And I want this to be forever. I know you're not where I am right now, and that's okay. I've wanted you for a long damn time."

"That's what you've said."

He shrugs. "It's my truth. I can feel it here." He places his hand over his chest, and my heart races as if it has a direct connection to his. "We can go the distance, and maybe you're right, maybe we can't," he's quick to add. "But I want to find out. I want to give this thing between us everything I've got. I want to know at the end of this, if there has to be an end, that I gave you one-hundred-percent of me. If you make me walk away, I want to know it's without regrets."

"When I tell you that I'm a mess, Maddox, I mean it. There is so much about me, my past, my fears, my inexperience." I let that confession hang between us. "I hate to see you get your hopes up and then be disappointed."

"Never." He stands and walks to the sink, rinsing out his cup before coming to stand next to me. He pulls me into his arms and rests his chin on my head. "I could never be disappointed in you, Brogan. Give it all to me—your past, your fears, and your inexperience. Add in the inability to trust too. I want it all, baby. I'll prove to you that you are not broken. You are not damaged, and you're not a mess. What you are is my wife, my beautiful wife."

"I want to believe that," I say, my voice cracking with emotion. It's been one hell of a rollercoaster the last couple of days.

"Do you want to come with me to my place?"

I don't know what I was expecting him to say, but changing the subject isn't it. I guess I assumed he'd keep trying to convince me that we're not fucking this up.

"Do you want me to come with you?"

"You're my wife now, Brogan. You've got shotgun no matter where I am. I don't care where I'm going or who I'm with. It will always be a better time if you're with me."

"Is there a book you read or something?" I ask him.

"What?" he asks, releasing his hold on me.

"What to say to make her melt? Swoon-worthy one-liners? *Capture her heart: Say the right things*? Come on, you can tell me. In fact, you should offer copies at the shop. That author deserves praise for his or her work."

He's grinning, which in turn makes me smile. Trust me, you can't have Maddox Lanigan turning that wide smile and those baby blues on you and not smile back at him. I've tried, and it's pretty much impossible.

He smacks my ass, making me yelp, and his smile grows. "New rule in the Lanigan house," he says, his smile lighting up his big blue eyes, while my belly flips as he refers to the home we're sharing as the Lanigan house. "We no longer talk about this not working. We both give it everything we've got. No, 'in six months' talk. It's us. That's it."

I think about what he's proposing, and I nod. I don't want to be a negative Nelly all the time, and he deserves me to give him this, even though I already know how it's going to go. "Okay."

"Good." He bends and tosses me over his shoulder, and I shriek with laughter. "Let's get ready, and I can take my wife to breakfast before we move me in."

"I can walk."

"I know you can, Mrs. Lanigan, but I like my hands on you." He carries me to my room. Make that "our" room, and tosses me gently on the bed.

I'm laughing.

He's smiling down at me.

Something a lot like hope flares in my chest. Maybe, just maybe, we can do this.

"You can bring whatever you want," I tell Maddox a few hours later. We're at his place, and so far, all I've seen him pack are clothes and toiletries.

"I'm a simple man, baby. I don't need much."

"It's supposed to be your home too, Maddox," I remind him.

"This house is small. I'm a minimalist at best. I'll box up my PlayStation and some photos." He nods to a frame that has him standing between an older couple.

"Are those your parents?" It has to be. The three of them are smiling widely, and a pang of sadness hits me. I miss my parents so much.

"It is. Hank and Cassie Lanigan, and their pride and joy, of course," he teases, pointing to his chest.

"So modest," I tease back.

He stalks toward me and wraps an arm around my waist, lifting me in the air. My body is molded to his as he holds my gaze. "I'm your favorite too. Admit it," he says, leaning in close.

Is he going to kiss me?

I lick my lips, and his eyes move to watch the action. "Say it, baby. Say I'm your favorite."

"I mean, top ten," I goad him.

"Brogan," he growls.

"Maddox." I pitch my voice to sound all deep and sexy like his, but I fail miserably, and we both fall into a fit of laughter.

He leans in and kisses the corner of my mouth, and I suck in a quick breath at the action. "One day, baby. One day you'll admit it's me. I'm your favorite. None of this top ten bullshit. Just your husband sitting next to you, holding that number one spot."

"We'll see," I taunt.

He shakes his head and slowly lowers me back to the floor. My body slides down his, and I feel his erection, but I pretend like I don't. I turn away, trying to hide, I'm sure, my tomato face, but my husband, he's tenacious and won't hear of letting me hide in my bubble. His arm that is still around my waist holds me to him while the other lifts my chin so that our eyes connect.

"That's all you, Brogan."

"Um, that's all you," I say, feeling even more heat rise to my cheeks.

He grins. Damn, that grin and those straight white teeth are a lethal combination. "Let me rephrase. That's all because of you. Only you." He kisses the tip of my nose before releasing his hold on me.

"Damn swoon book," I grumble, loud enough that he can hear me. He tosses his head back in laughter, and I love the sound. Maddox is a laid-back guy. He's easy to like and fun to be around.

The next six months won't be lonely, but I have a feeling the after will be worse than when Briar and the girls moved out. Only time will tell.

Once we have his truck packed up, it's close to time that he needs to be at the shop. "Take my car," I offer. "I'll drive your truck to the house and get everything unloaded."

"I don't want you lugging in all of this."

"Well, what do you suggest? You have to be at the shop in forty minutes."

He ponders this for a few minutes. "How about I just pull my truck into the garage? That way it's not out in the weather, and you take me to work, and I can get one of the guys to drop me off after work, and then I'll be home."

"I can pick you up too," I offer. It feels like the right thing to do.

"Nah, I don't want you out on the roads after dark. It's supposed to snow. I'm sure one of the guys will drop me off."

"Okay. Well, you better get moving. We'll hit a drive-thru and get you some food to scarf down before you have to start. I don't need you passing out while trying to mark someone's skin permanently."

"Babe, you do realize it's only the person getting ink that gets lightheaded, right?" he asks, humor lacing his tone.

"Yeah, yeah, let's go, Lanigan."

"Yes, ma'am." He rushes to pull his truck into his detached garage while I make my way through the house, turning off the lights, and locking the door. I meet him at my car, and he opens the door for me. It's on the tip of my tongue to remind him that he doesn't need to do that, but it'll be wasted words. Instead, I smile and say, "Thank you," as I slide behind the wheel.

Thirty minutes later, I pull up outside the shop to drop him off. He's got his food in his hands when he leans over and kisses my cheek. "Let me know you make it home. Thank you for the ride."

"Wives give their husbands a ride to work sometimes, right?" I shrug like it's no big deal, but the smile on Maddox's face tells me that it is. "What's with the cheesy smile?"

"You called me your husband." He winks and climbs out of the car. I don't pull away until I see that he's inside. The entire drive home, I'm lost in thought. Today was good. I enjoy spending time with him. I'm also excited for him to come home to me.

I'm in so much trouble.

MADDOX 6

STEPPING INTO THE SHOP WITH a bag of fast food in my hand feels different. I've done this exact thing more times than I can count, but this time, I'm a married man. A married man that ignores the two ladies in the waiting room making eyes at me. I pretend like I don't see them. I'm not interested.

Just like that.

Overnight, my world has changed, and I'm embracing it. "Hey," I greet Drake, who is working at the front desk today. "I still have a two o'clock, right?" I ask.

He glances down at the computer. "Still on the books. No calls yet, and they're not here."

We don't have no-shows often, but we do require a deposit to schedule, and if they are a no-show, that deposit is nonrefundable. It helps offset the loss of income. However, we all have waiting lists, and our number of walk-ins grows every day. Some more than others. Today, though, I'm good with my client not showing up. That means I get to go home to my wife earlier than expected.

"There he is!" Lachlan says, stepping out of his office, following a client to the front desk to check out. He shakes his client's hand and follows me into my office. "How's married life?" he asks, amusement in his tone.

"Fucking fantastic." I grin as I pull food out of the bag.

"And then there was one." He laughs.

I shrug. "How's your day been?"

"Fine as frog hair. That was my last client of the day. My afternoon rescheduled."

"You taking walk-ins?" I ask, biting into my burger.

"I might. Drake said there were two out in the waiting room. What about you?"

"My two o'clock isn't here yet. If they don't show, I'm going back home. Which reminds me, I'm going to need a ride to my place."

"Your place or Brogan's?"

"Mine. I packed up my things today to move in, but left my truck parked in the garage. I didn't have time to unload it, and I didn't want it sitting outside in the weather. Brogan offered to drive it home for me, but I know she'd be trying to unload it all for me, and I don't want her lifting all those heavy-ass boxes. It's mostly clothes, but still."

"You called her place home."

"That's where she is. That's home."

"Damn, you've got it bad, huh?"

"I've wanted her for a long time, Lach. I thought it would complicate things between our group with Forrest and Briar getting married, but when I woke up next to her... when I found out she was my wife, well, I changed my mind. She's already mine, so I convinced her that we give this a shot."

"Yeah? You're going for it."

I nod. "With everything I got."

"Well, if you're anything like the first three, I'm certain you'll come out with a win."

"Just her. Win or lose, I just want her. I know we can make this work."

"Make what work?" Roman asks from the doorway of my office.

"My marriage."

Roman nods. "I'm an old pro. Hit me up if you need any advice."

"Who needs advice?" Legend asks, stepping into the room next to Roman.

Before I can answer, Forrest joins in. "What is this? A meeting without me?"

"What are you doing here?" I ask him. "You're supposed to be at home with your wife and daughters."

Forrest grins. "My girls are just fine, thank you very much. I ran out to grab everything we need to make homemade potato soup because Briar's been craving it and thought I'd stop in to see how everything's going."

"Is she pregnant?" Roman asks.

"Nah, but if she were, that would be fucking amazing." Forrest's smile grows, thinking about expanding their family.

"Well, you're just in time. I was telling Maddox if he needs any marriage advice to come see me." Roman fills him and Legend in on our conversation.

"Me too," Legend speaks up.

"I'm new at this," Forrest admits, "but I'm here if you need to talk."

"Thanks." I nod, making eye contact with my four best friends. "We're giving this a shot. I have six months to make her fall in love with me."

"Meh, you won't need six weeks." Legend waves his hand in the air.

"Right? It's obvious there's chemistry," Roman agrees.

"Love me. I need to make her fall *in* love with me."

"Just be you, Mad. Brogan is a lot like Briar. They value trust over everything, and it takes a good pair of hiking boots and a lot of fucking resilience to scale that mountain, but when you do, I promise you that you'll have no regrets," Forrest says.

"Thanks, man."

"Hey, Maddox, your client just canceled. Car trouble. I worked him back in, but it's not for a few months from now. He was fine with that. Do you want walk-ins today?" Drake asks, stepping into the now crowded room.

"No. I'm going home to my wife."

Drake's eyes widen, and I laugh. "I guess these jokers didn't tell you that Forrest wasn't the only one who got married over the weekend."

"They did not. Who's the lucky girl?" Drake asks.

"Brogan." I'm smiling just from saying her name, but I can't seem to help myself.

"No shit. A double wedding to twin sisters?"

"Not exactly, but yeah, two weddings, and twin sisters." I raise my hand and wiggle my ring finger, showing him the proof. This ring already feels like it's a part of me, as if I've been wearing it for years.

"I didn't even know you and Brogan were dating," Drake comments.

"Well, now, we're married." I don't bother to tell him we weren't. He'll figure it out, and if not, that's fine too. She's my wife, and she's going to stay my wife, so how we came to be married is a non-issue at this stage in the game.

"I better get these groceries home."

"Hey, man, you mind dropping by my place?" I ask Forrest. "My truck is loaded with my things and in the garage. I ran out of time to take it home before I had to come in today."

"Sure. You ready now?"

"Yep." I gather my trash from the food I inhaled and toss it into the can. "We're out," I tell my friends.

"Enjoy the honeymoon, fellas!" Roman calls after us.

"Don't want to hear about yours!" Forrest calls back to Roman, making us all laugh.

"You can't push her too hard," Forrest says once we're in his truck.

"I know. But I can fight for both of us while she's taking the time to get caught up to where I am with this."

"They're a lot alike, and therapy has helped, but there are still old scars that will take some time to heal."

"I know."

"My wife is happy about this union of yours. She thinks you'll be good for Brogan."

His words take root in my mind, and I let them wash over me. Her sister thinks I'm good for her. The fact of the matter is that Brogan is good for me too. I feel lighter than I have in years, just knowing that as soon as I get into my truck, I'm going home to her. I've never had someone to come home to, and damn, it's a feeling like nothing else.

"She's good for me," I finally answer as he pulls his truck into the driveway.

"Happy for you, man."

"You too. Tell the girls, all three of them, I said hello."

"You and Brogan should come to dinner one night. My wife would love to see her sister, and you too."

"We'll do that. Let me talk to my wife, and I'll let you know."

He chuckles. "You think we'll ever get tired of saying it?"

"Not if Roman and Legend are our examples. Thanks for the lift, man."

"Anytime."

Hopping out of the truck, I don't even bother going into the house. I head straight for the detached garage, entering through the side entry door and start my truck. I sit inside and shiver until it's warm, and pull out, hit the garage door opener, and head toward home.

When I get halfway home, I know I need to turn around. I need to tell my parents I'm married, and that's a conversation we need to have face-to-face. Fifteen minutes later, I'm pulling into their driveway. I keep the truck running because I don't plan to stay long. My wife is waiting for me, and I'm anxious to get home to her.

"Mom! Dad!" I call out as I step through the door. I don't bother knocking because my parents have told me more times than I can count that I don't need to—that this will always be my home.

"In the kitchen!" Dad calls back.

I stride down the hall and step into the kitchen to see Mom sitting at the island while Dad slices a loaf of homemade bread. "Hey." I hug my mom and kiss her cheek.

"What brings you here?" she asks, returning my hug.

"Oh, you know, I thought I should drop in to tell you that I got married."

Dad stops what he's doing and his eyes find mine. "For real?"

I nod. "Yeah, she's incredible."

"We didn't even know you were dating anyone," Mom says.

"I wasn't." I go on to tell her how I've been interested in Brogan for months and why I never took my shot.

"You always take the shot, son," Dad tells me after I've explained my current situation.

"I know, and the one time I didn't, I regretted it. I learned from that mistake."

"How does she feel about all of this? Your wife, Brogan, right?" Mom clarifies.

"Yeah, Brogan," I say, not holding back the smile just saying her name brings to my face. "She's worried I'll change my mind. She has a past that's shaped her feelings. She wants this to work."

Mom nods. "When do we get to meet her?"

"Soon, but I'm going to leave that up to her. I'm going to give her some time before I bring it up. I need to get going. She's at home waiting for me."

"And where is home?" Dad asks.

"Wherever she is," I answer automatically.

"Good answer, son. Give your wife our best, and let her know we can't wait to meet her, but she can take all the time she needs."

"It's poetic, really," Mom says. "We met and fell in love quickly. You grew up hearing our love story; it's only natural you'd have one similar."

Love.

"Love you, Mom."

"Love you too."

"Hey!" Dad pretends to pout.

"Love you too, old man." I wave, and then I'm rushing out the door. Rushing home to my wife.

At the front door with a bouquet of flowers in hand, I hesitate. This is my home now, but am I supposed to knock? Deciding to just walk on in, I turn the handle and call out, "Honey, I'm home!" Kicking off my shoes, I go in search of my wife.

I find her in the living room curled up with a blanket, watching TV. "Hey. You're back early."

"Yeah, my client canceled, so I stopped by my parents' and then came straight home." I sit next to her on the couch and lean in to kiss her cheek. "These are for you."

"What? You bought me flowers?"

"I did."

"Why?" She glances from the flowers in my hands back to me.

"Can a husband not buy flowers for his wife?" I ask, tilting my head to the side. I study her and watch as tears well in her eyes. This was meant to be a good surprise, not one to cause her tears.

"I don't know," she answers. "My dad, he was only with my mom, and she passed away when we were babies."

My fucking chest cracks, seeing the sadness and hearing her talk about all that she's lost. "Well, life is what we make it. I've never been a husband before, but I wanted to bring my wife flowers. Not because I want something or need to apologize. I just wanted to make you smile."

She flashes me a watery grin and reaches for the bouquet. She smells them before replying softly, "Thank you, Maddox."

"You're welcome. Let me put them in water for you, and then I'll start packing all of my things in."

"I can do it."

"Finish your movie," I tell her.

"It's a rerun of a Christmas movie. I've already seen it." She tosses the cover off her lap, and stands, making her way to the kitchen. I follow her and watch as she pulls open the cabinet doors and searches. "I don't know if I have something to put them in." She rummages some more and comes up with a plastic pitcher. "This will have to do."

"I'll do better next time," I tell her. I'm already kicking myself in the ass for not buying the huge bouquet with the vase. I didn't even think about her needing one.

"There," she says, stepping back to survey her work. "Thank you, Maddox. They're beautiful, and I'll always remember the first time I ever got flowers." She pulls her phone out of her pocket and snaps a picture.

"Perfect." I wink.

"You went to see your parents?"

"Yeah, I thought I should tell them in person that I got married."

"How did that go?" she asks. I can hear the worry in her voice.

"Good." I nod. "They trust me, and I told them how amazing you are. They can't wait to meet you."

"Can we maybe give it a little more time?"

"Absolutely." I smile, letting her know I mean what I say. She can take all the time she needs. Sure, my parents are eager to meet her, but I explained our situation and told them we needed some time. I knew Brogan wasn't ready yet. "I'm going to go grab some boxes." I need to step away before I grab her and haul her off to our room to do things I know she's not ready for. Something about knowing that I'm the first man to treat this woman like the queen she is lights a fire inside my soul. I want all of her firsts, everything she's never had or experienced. I want her to share all of them with me.

"Let me get my shoes on."

"Why don't you just stand by the door and hold it open for me? That way, we're not letting all of the heat out. I don't have too many and it's cold as hell outside."

"I have a coat and boots." She laughs.

"Yeah, but you're all warm and snuggly in here. Just watch for me and open the door." I place a kiss on her temple, move back to the front door to slide into my shoes, and head outside to grab my things.

Thirty minutes later, my hands are like ice cubes, even with my gloves. My cheeks are red, my lips feel chapped, and my ears are numb, but all of my things are in the house.

"So, I cleaned out a couple of drawers for you and some space in the closet. I assumed you didn't want to take Briar's old room?" She laughs nervously.

"Nah, not unless you plan on moving in there with me."

"Come on back. I'll show you." She turns to move down the hall, and I follow her with a box in my hands. "That dresser. I gave you the left-side three drawers, and then the left side of the closet too."

"What did you do with all of your things?"

"I was long overdue for a closet clean out."

"Fair enough. I'll get this unpacked and we can talk about what we're going to make for dinner."

"Oh, I can handle dinner."

"Brogan, this is a partnership. I don't expect you to do all the cooking and cleaning. Just go relax and we'll figure it out together. You're not my maid. You're my wife."

"Together." She nods and leaves the room.

I get busy unpacking the first two boxes when she appears with another in her arms. "I'm helping so shush it," she says, before I can tell her she doesn't need to help me. It's not because I don't want her in here with me or that I have anything to hide. I don't want her to think that she has to help me.

"How was the rest of your day?" I ask, as we work to fold and hang up clothes.

"Good. I came home and did some cleaning, as you know, and had only been sitting for maybe ten minutes when you got here."

"You went through your clothes fast."

"Yeah, it's easy. If I have not worn it in ages, and have no desire to, it went to the donate pile."

I hold up a shirt that fits that description perfectly. "Where is this donate pile?" I ask, wadding up the shirt.

She points to the corner of the room where three large clothes baskets sit filled to the brim. I toss my shirt into one of the baskets and keep working. Together, we make quick work of getting me moved in, and the donate pile grows by another full basket.

"Thank you," I say, pulling her into my arms, and hugging her tightly. "Now, let's eat. I've worked up an appetite." Releasing her from my hold, I lace my fingers with hers and lead us to the kitchen. "What sounds good to you?" I ask her.

"Honestly, tuna casserole. I've been craving it. Do you eat tuna?"

"Yep. I'm not a picky eater. I've never made it, so tell me what I need to do."

"I can make it."

"You can, and we can also make it together. Teach me your ways." I bow to her, making her laugh.

"Okay, I'll grab the ingredients. We need a baking dish and a mixing bowl. Both are in those cabinets." She points to the lower cabinets next to the stove as she makes her way to the other side of the kitchen to grab the ingredients.

"What now?"

"Well, we open and drain the tuna, which is the worst part, but this is so good."

"I can handle that." I grab the two cans of tuna and get to work.

"Now dump them in the bowl, and I usually rinse the can out with soapy water so it's not stinking up the entire house for days."

"Good thinking." I do as she suggests, and then toss the cans. She's already got a mixture of the rest of the ingredients going into the bowl.

"What now?"

She instructs me, and we work in tandem to make dinner. "How long should I set the timer for?" I ask, sliding the casserole dish into the oven.

"Twenty minutes."

"Great. I'll wash up these dishes while it cooks. Go finish your movie."

"Maddox"—she shakes her head—"it was one I've seen before."

"Fine, pick one out for us to watch after dinner."

"You want to watch a movie with me?"

"I do."

"And you're letting me choose?"

"I am. Why is that so surprising?"

"Aren't men supposed to command the remote?"

I shrug. "Not me. I don't give a single fuck what's playing on that screen as long as I'm snuggled up with you."

"You've been reading your swoon manual again, I see." She smiles, and turns on her heel, heading to the living room.

"There is no manual!" I call after her.

"I call bullshit, Lanigan. There is no man on this planet with lines that smooth all on his own."

I chuckle to myself as I take care of the dishes and wipe down the counter. I have just enough time to pour us both a glass of sweet tea and carry them to the living room when the timer goes off.

"I'll be right back with our plates."

"I can make mine."

"Let me take care of you, Brogan." I see indecision on her face, but she eventually nods and settles back onto the couch. Dipping out two helpings of dinner, I grab two forks, some napkins, and make my way back to her.

"Thank you."

"This is so good," I say, after taking my first bite. She beams at me, and that's how we eat the first meal we cooked together as husband and wife.

"I'll take care of these," she says, taking my empty bowl out of my hands. "Do you want more?"

"No, I'm stuffed. Did you see how full my bowl was?"

"Let me clean up and I'll be in for the movie."

"I'm going to grab a quick shower." I'm all sweaty from lifting those boxes. I rush through my shower because I have a cuddle movie date with my wife.

I find her in the living room, with the remote in hand, and both of our glasses of tea refilled.

"Ready?"

"Not yet." I take a seat on the opposite end of the couch. "Come here." She raises her brow in question, but does as I ask, and moves closer. I pull her into my arms, and drape the blanket over her lap. "Now I'm ready."

I don't know what I expected, but it's not her relaxing into me and starting the movie. If this is what the next fifty or so years are going to be like, I hope time drags so I can enjoy every second with her.

BROGAN 7

I'VE CHANGED MY OUTFIT THREE times, and the bedroom looks like a bomb exploded. I don't know why I'm this nervous. I've had dinner with my sister and her daughters at Forrest's place, which is now their home, more times than I can count since they moved.

This time shouldn't be any different.

I keep telling myself this, but I'm still stressing about it. It's the first time Maddox and I will be attending anything with our friends and family since being married a week ago today. The morning after at the hotel doesn't count. I was still firmly in the "we're getting this annulled" camp at the time. Now, well, I've agreed to give him six months, and a week in, I know my husband is not against playing dirty.

The things this man says. He melts my insides. We're talking swoon all the way, and I can't tell if he's playing a game, or if that's just really him. My heart tells me that's just Maddox in a relationship, but my head, that bastard tells me I can't trust it. It's going to be a long six months.

"Whoa."

I look up to find Maddox standing in the doorway of the bedroom. The one we now share. "Sorry." I wince.

He steps inside and doesn't stop until he has his arms wrapped around me. "What's going on in that pretty head of yours?"

"I'm trying to find something to wear," I mumble against his chest. Something I've learned over the last week about my new husband is that he's a touchy-feely guy, and he loves hugs. Not only does he love them, but he's damn good at it. It's been a week, and already his arms around me have a calming effect, like nothing I've ever felt before.

"You'd look beautiful in a paper sack."

"Stop." I playfully swat at his chest.

"Tell me what's really going on, Brogan?" His voice is soft, soothing almost.

I exhale loudly, but I don't pull away from his hold. "It's the first time we're doing something with other people since the morning we woke up married."

"And?"

"And... I don't know. I'm just... nervous, I guess."

"You have nothing to be nervous about." He pulls back and places his index finger beneath my chin so that I have to look at him. "You and me, Brogan. That's how we face this. Together. I'm your huckleberry, baby. If you want to leave at any time, we will, but, baby, this is our future. You don't go to these things alone anymore. And it doesn't matter what you're wearing. Everyone is going to be happy to see you. You're the same Brogan you were two weeks ago, only now, you're also a wife. My wife, and trust me, there isn't a single piece of clothing in this house that you would look bad in." He bends and kisses the tip of my nose.

"Yeah, yeah," I mutter, feeling mollified at his response. I pull out of his arms and look down at the black leggings and oversized sweater I'm wearing. I guess this will have to do. I know I'm freaking out for nothing, but I don't know how to stop it.

"You're beautiful, Brogan."

I look up to find him watching me intently. There is nothing but honesty staring back at me, and that look, the one I'm learning to know and trust, mends another small broken piece of me. "I just need to grab my shoes and I'm ready to go. I'll deal with all of this"—I wave my arms around the room—"when we get back."

"I'll help you when we get back. The truck is already running, and I put the brownies you made for the girls in the back seat."

"Thank you, but I could have gotten them."

"I know, but I was heading out to the truck, anyway." He moves toward the bedroom door. "I'll be in the living room when you're ready. Take your time." He gives me a smile that feels kind of like a fist reaching into my chest and squeezing my heart.

Once in my closet, I grab my black ankle booties and shove my feet into them. I don't bother looking in the mirror. I've done that enough today already. Maddox is right. This is my sister, and my nieces, and my brother-in-law. They're not going to judge me or judge us. The only judgment I'm going to get is avoiding my sister's calls or cutting them short all week, telling her I had to get back to work. Not a complete lie, but I wasn't ready to talk about my current situation. I'm still not ready, but I can't avoid her forever.

"Good choice," Maddox says when I enter the living room. He stands from the couch and holds my coat open for me. I know better than to tell him I can put my coat on by myself. Instead, I smile, say, "Thank you," and slide into my coat with his help.

"You want me to carry you to the truck so you don't get your boots in the snow?"

"What? No." I chuckle. "They're boots."

"They look fancy. I think I should."

Before I know what's happening, Maddox has me in his arms, bridal style, just as he did the day we got home from Vegas a week ago and carries me out to the truck. "I can get the door," I tell him when we reach the passenger side.

Somehow, we manage to pull open the door, and he sets me inside on the seat. I open my mouth to say thank you, because what else can I say? But he surprises me when he leans in and pulls my seat belt across my chest and latches it.

"I'm going to go lock the house. Be right back." He drops a kiss to my cheek, shuts the door, and jogs off toward the house.

I was so lost in being in his arms I didn't even think about the front door not being shut. That's what he does to me. He scrambles my brain and makes me forget who I am and how to act. Case in point, waking up married after a drunken night in Vegas. Maddox Lanigan has super powers.

"Stay there," Maddox says as he parks his truck in Forrest and Briar's driveway.

"You are not carrying me to the house," I scold him.

He grins. "I just want to get your door."

"I can do it. You don't have to treat me like glass, Maddox. It's going to be a long six months for you if you do."

He turns to face me. His expression is hard. "I'm not treating you like glass, Brogan. I'm treating you like my wife. With the respect that you deserve, nothing more, nothing less. And it's going to be a long, happy life of me taking care of you, treating you the way you deserve to be treated. You might as well go ahead and get used to it. I'm not going to stop now or in fifty years from now."

He doesn't wait for me to reply, which is good because I'm speechless. I wouldn't know how to respond to that if I tried. Instead, he removes his keys from the ignition and climbs out of the truck. I remain seated just as he asked me to while he comes to my side to open the door. He opens the back door first and grabs the container of brownies, before closing it and opening mine. He offers me his free hand, and I take it, allowing him to help me down from the truck.

His hand rests on the small of my back as he leads us to the front door. He doesn't knock. Instead, he twists the handle and shouts, "We're here!" The pitter-patter of giggles and little feet fill the room, and there they are. River and Rayne cheer and launch themselves at me. I barely have time to kneel to accept their hugs.

"Aunt Brogan, we missed you," Rayne says.

"I missed you, too." I hug them tightly, one twin in each arm, until they wiggle free, and move on to Maddox.

"Uncle Maddox!" They have just as much excitement for my new husband as they do for me. It's not because we're married now. Maddox has been in their life as their uncle as long as Forrest has. To them, there is no difference.

To be young again.

Maddox kneels to hug them one at a time because he still has the container of brownies in his hands. "Where are your mom and dad?" Maddox asks them.

"In the kitchen. Let's go!" Rayne takes his free hand, and River takes her sister's as they start to drag Maddox off toward the kitchen.

I stare after them, grateful for all the new people in our lives. None of them blinked an eye at accepting those girls as Forrest's daughters. They've embraced all four of us into their lives, and ours are more enriched having met them.

Maddox looks back at me over his shoulder. "Coming, babe?"

"Yeah." I nod, because my voice is so soft I'm not sure he can hear me. The emotions are thick in my throat, but I swallow them down and prepare myself for my sister's inquisition.

"You made it!" Briar says as soon as we enter the kitchen. She comes rushing toward me and pulls me into a hug. "I've missed you this week." She gives me a knowing look, and I shrug.

"Uncle Maddox, what's that?" River asks, pointing to the container of brownies. I'm surprised they've just now noticed them.

"Aunt Brogan made these for you." He opens the lid so that they can see inside.

"She did?" the twins ask in unison.

"She did, but you have to eat all your dinner if you want one of these delicious brownies."

"We love brownies," Rayne tells him.

"Me too." He winks, places the lid back on the container, and sets it on the counter.

"What can I help with?" I ask my sister.

"Nothing, it's all done. Forrest made white chicken chili in the Crock-Pot, so we kind of cheated, I guess." She smiles.

River gasps. "Daddy! You're not supposed to cheat."

Forrest grins as he bends and scoops River into his arms. "Razzle, you're right. Cheating is bad. What Mommy meant was we made an easy meal, so it wasn't a lot of work."

River furrows her brow, but before she can reply, her sister is stealing the show.

"Daddy, chili's not supposed to be white." She places her little hands on her hips and gives him her best four-going-on-fourteen attitude.

Maddox lifts Rayne onto his hip and takes her to the Crock-Pot, and lifts the lid. "They call it chili because of the beans, but it's kind of more like a chicken soup. See." He puts the ladle in and scoops up a helping to show her.

"Sissy, adults are weird," Rayne tells River.

They fall into a fit of giggles, but that could have more to do with Forrest and Maddox tickling them for calling them weird than with their own assessment.

"Let's eat, then I'm stealing your wife," Briar tells Maddox.

He glances over at me, and his eyes soften. "That's fine, but just know I'm not leaving here without her." He tosses me a flirty wink before turning his attention back to Rayne as if he didn't just melt my heart into a puddle in the middle of my sister's kitchen floor.

"Damn," Briar mutters. She loops her arm through mine. "That was hot as hell, and total book boyfriend vibes."

"I think he has a book or some kind of manual. He keeps saying all the right things."

"Hmmm, maybe my husband and your husband are reading the same book then." She chuckles. "They're just good guys, Brogan. Good men, who I know our father would have approved of."

"Yours maybe. Not mine."

"What do you mean? Maddox is great."

"We weren't even dating, Briar."

"*Pft*, who cares. This is your life, and you live it how you want. You know that's what Susan would tell you. Have you talked to her about any of this?"

"No. I have an appointment with her next week."

"Do you need me to go with you?"

"Thank you, but no. I'll be fine."

"Have you considered having Maddox go to an appointment with you? You know he'd go. When Forrest went with me, it was a great visit."

"He was already in love with you and you with him by that point."

"And you're crazy if you think that man isn't falling in love with you." She points to where Maddox is standing talking to Forrest. He glances over and smiles at me before giving his attention back to his friend.

"He can't go five seconds without looking over to see where you are."

"He's just hungry," I tell her.

"My dear, dear sister, you are in denial. Come on, let's eat." She guides me back to the center of the kitchen, where the girls are already eating at the island. "Girls, let's move you into the dining room so we can all eat together," Briar tells them.

I get lost in her words, one in particular. Denial. I trust Briar more than anyone, and maybe she's right. Maybe it's not because he's hungry, or maybe it is. Maybe he's just hungry for me?

"Daddy said we could eat here," River says, pulling me out of my thoughts.

"Razzle," Forrest says gently. "I said you could eat there until Mommy and Aunt Brogan were ready to join us."

"Please, Daddy?" Rayne sticks her bottom lip out in a pout.

Forrest looks to Briar, his eyes pleading. She shakes her head. He's such a pushover when it comes to the girls.

"Don't you want to eat at the table with the rest of us like big girls?" Maddox asks them.

"We're big." River squares her shoulders, and Maddox chuckles.

"Come on. I'll give you a ride." He turns and offers River his back, and she latches on.

"Hop on, sweetheart." Forrest does the same for Rayne, and the girls giggle and laugh for the whole twenty steps or fewer it takes to get to the dining room.

Briar and I grab their food and cups and get them all set up before we make our own. The girls carry the conversation as we eat. Mostly that it's weird that we call what we're eating chili because it's not red.

These two, they always manage to make me smile, and I miss them so much. I'm glad Maddox suggested we get together. It's eerie how well he already knows what I need without me having to tell him.

"We'll clean up," Forrest says, when Briar stands and reaches for my bowl. "You two go get caught up. We've got this, and the girls."

"Oh, Uncle Maddox, wanna play with us? Daddy said we could play salon and paint his nails." River bounces in her seat.

"Sure," Maddox says, holding his hand out for her to see. "What color are you thinking?"

"We gots lots of colors, Uncle Maddox."

"Finish your dinner," Forrest says, smiling at them. "Then we're all yours."

"Thanks, babe," Briar tells her husband.

"Never thank me for taking care of our daughters, Briar."

I lean over and whisper in my sister's ear, "I think that was in the manual too." The words are barely out of my mouth before Briar is cracking up laughing.

"We'll be in the basement." She grabs my hand and tugs for me to follow her. Once we're settled on the couch, with the television on for noise to drown out our conversation, she gives me a pointed look.

"What do you want me to say?"

"Anything. Everything. I know you well enough to know you're hiding within yourself. You're still married, and the last text message you sent me said we're seeing where it goes."

Sitting back on the couch, I close my eyes. "He asked me to give him six months." I take a few minutes and replay that conversation in my head, just as I have every day since it took place. Finally, I open my eyes and glance over at my sister. "He says that in six months, neither one of us will want to walk away. Briar, when we got here, he told me to stay put. I thought he wanted to carry me to the house, like he has before."

"Wait. Hold up. He carries you to the house?"

"Well, I mean, he carried me inside that first day when we got home from Vegas, and again because he didn't want me to walk in the snow." My face heats as I explain this to my sister.

"Damn," she mutters. "Maddox is a dreamboat."

"Stop." I swat at her arm, laughing. "Anyway, I told him he didn't have to carry me and he said he just wanted to open my door for me. Then I spouted off how he doesn't need to treat me like glass because this is all new to me, Briar. I've seen what happens in the movies and on TV. I see how Forrest, Roman, and Legend treat you, Emerson, and Monroe, but I have no first-hand experience myself, and honestly, I feel like I'm living a damn fairy tale, and I'm waiting for the credits to roll, and for it to all be over."

"I know that feeling, but, Brogan, this is real life. We've had our share of pain. It took me some time to realize that our past doesn't define our future."

"Okay, now you sound like Susan."

"Thank you." Briar nods, and I smile. I really did need this time with my sister. "So, what did he say to you, telling him he didn't have to treat you like glass?"

"Something about how he's treating me like his wife, not glass, and that I better get used to it because it's going to be the standard for the next fifty or so years."

"Damn," Briar says, her mouth hanging open. "He's got a way with words, that one."

"See! That's what I mean. How can I trust him when he's that smooth?"

"Brogan," Briar says gently. "You can trust him. He cares about you. Anyone can see that. To hear Emerson and Monroe tell it, these guys, when they fall, they fall hard, and they turn into giant teddy bears for the women in their lives. I know Forrest did. You see how Roman and Legend are with their wives. That's what he knows. That's who he is. It's not fake."

"Not so long ago, you would have been agreeing with me," I grumble, crossing my arms over my chest.

"I know. It took me a lot of time, and Forrest gave me as much as I needed to come to terms with the fact that he's one of the good ones. He's not all pretty words and no actions. Let Maddox show you."

"I told him I'd give him six months, but, Briar, I'm already— it's going to hurt when he leaves. I'm broken, and when he realizes that, he's going to bolt, and my heart... it won't ever be the same."

Briar pulls me into a hug. "You are not broken. That night can't define us."

"Everyone I love leaves me." The words slip free before I can stop them.

"No. I didn't leave you." Her tone is firm, one she uses with the girls when she means business. "I'm right here. I'm just a short drive away and no matter when you need me, day or night, I'm going to be there. Our family is growing, and sure, the girls and I don't live with you anymore, but that's okay because you'll have kids one day; I'm certain that husband of yours will make sure of it."

"I've never—he's more experienced than me. He's not going to want a wife who doesn't know what she's doing in bed. He's had his fair share of women. He's not going to want to choose a novice to sex to have sleep next to him for the rest of his life."

"You're wrong." She points to her chest. "I was the same way, remember? I don't have a single memory from that night at the frat party. In every way that matters, Forrest was my first. Don't stress about the small things. Talk to him, tell him, and I promise you, he's not going to disappoint you. Neither will your body," she assures me.

"I'm scared," I admit. "And yes, before you ask me if I've told him that, I have. He says he won't hurt me."

"Then put your faith in him, Brogan."

"But what if I'm right?"

"Then I'll be here for you to help you pick up the pieces, but my gut tells me that you're wrong. What is your gut telling you?"

I clamp my mouth shut, which is the only answer she needs. It's not my gut or my heart that's the issue. It's my head. I can't seem to stop thinking about the what-ifs and just live for the here and now.

"Come, let's go spend some time with our family. I need to threaten my new brother-in-law."

"Please don't," I beg her, and she giggles all the way up the steps. "Briar," I say, grabbing her attention. She stops and turns to look at me. "Remember that tattoo we always talked about?"

Her eyes light up. "I do."

"Are you ready?"

She nods. "I think we waited for a reason. We were waiting for our husbands." She winks, and I smile as I follow her into the kitchen in search of the girls and our husbands.

We find everyone in the living room. River is painting Forrest's nails, and Rayne is painting Maddox's nails.

"Look!" they say in tandem.

Briar heads toward Forrest, and I do the same to Maddox. "Wow, you're doing a great job, Rayne," I tell my niece.

"Do I look pretty, baby?" Maddox asks, as he raises his left hand that's already painted. His wedding band catches my eyes, and my chest tightens. I ignore it and settle on the floor next to him.

"Handsome," I tell him.

Maddox reaches over and places his hand on my thigh. He gives a soft squeeze and leaves it to rest there while Rayne works on his other hand.

"I can do yours too, Aunt Brogan."

"After this it's bedtime," Briar tells the girls. "We'll have to plan another day for Aunt Brogan to come over so you can paint her nails. Maybe we'll even go to the salon and we can all get our nails painted."

"Daddy too?" River asks.

"No, a girls' day," Briar replies.

"Oh, we love girls' day!" Rayne exclaims.

The girls finish their job, and Maddox and Forrest make a huge deal about how great they did, and their little faces beam with pride.

"All right, little ladies, time for bed," Briar tells them.

"We should be heading out too." I stand and offer Maddox my hand, to help him do the same. Once he's on his feet, he wraps his arm around my waist and presses a kiss to my temple.

"Thank you for dinner, and the manicure," he says to the girls. "Our place next time?" he suggests.

"We'll be there," Forrest tells him.

After a round of hugs, we're heading out to the truck. Maddox opens the door for me, and this time, I smile and thank him. The drive home is quiet. Once back, we go through our nightly routine, and when Maddox turns off the light, he whispers my name.

"Brogan?"

"Yeah?"

"Come here, baby."

It's like this every night. I try to sleep on my side of the bed, but he insists that he holds me. Without a word, I move, and he meets me in the middle, wrapping his arms around me. He places a tender kiss on my shoulder. "Night, beautiful."

For the first time since we've been living together and sleeping in the same bed, I don't think about how I'm going to handle life when I no longer have him here. This time, I snuggle a little closer, and whisper, "Goodnight, Mad," before allowing myself to drift off to sleep.

MADDOX 8

It's Saturday, and Brogan has to work. She only works one weekend a month unless she's picking up hours. This is the first Saturday since we've been married that she's not been home, and I don't know what I'm going to do with myself.

I'm missing my wife.

I got up early and made her breakfast, which seemed to shock her. I believe her exact words were "Why would you be up this early on a weekend when you have nowhere to be?" I just smiled and handed her a plate of toast, bacon, and eggs. While she ate her breakfast, I started her car for her and filled her favorite tumbler with coffee, just the way she likes it.

She mentioned that she needed to go to the store, and I assured her that I could do it on my own. We've done the grocery shopping together every Saturday for a month. I'm sure I can handle it. Her face got an adorable shade of red when she told me she needed feminine products. I told her to text me what she needed, but she refused. So, I went to the bathroom and brought out the almost empty boxes. When I asked her if it was the right ones, she nodded and tucked her chin to her chest.

She's cute as hell, thinking that I wouldn't walk into any store and buy her what she needs. As soon as she left, I cleaned up the kitchen from breakfast, started a load of laundry, and swept and mopped the floors.

Looking around, I make a mental note to dust when I return. I want to head to the store so I can get back and make sure I have dinner ready when she gets home. I double check to make sure I have my phone, wallet, and the list from the refrigerator, and get on the road. As I'm driving through town, I get the idea to take her a little treat. I know she loves the vanilla chai lattes from Pastry Haven, which isn't far from her work.

I'm in and out in less than ten minutes and pulling into the lot of her work. I strut through the main doors like I own the place as my eyes scan behind the desk, looking for Brogan.

"Hi, can I help you?" an older lady greets me.

"I hope so. I was hoping to see my wife and give her a midmorning pick me up." I raise the latte so she can see it.

"Oh, that's so sweet. Who is your wife?"

"Brogan Lanigan." Damn, I love the sound of that. Her eyes widen, which tells me she probably has no idea we're married. Something like disappointment washes over me, but I push it back. I have five more months to make her want this, want me for a lifetime.

She recovers quickly. "Oh! Brogan. Let me get her." She rolls her chair back as she stands and disappears into the back of the office. I stand off to the side, not wanting to be in anyone's way, when the door to the lobby opens, and Brogan sticks her head out.

"Maddox? What are you doing here?"

"I brought you a vanilla chai latte." I hand her the cup as I lean in to kiss her cheek. I know she's at work, but I can't help myself where my wife is concerned.

"That was sweet of you. You didn't have to do that."

"I wanted to. I'm on my way to the store, so it wasn't out of the way."

She nods, taking a sip of her drink. "It's perfect, Maddox. Thank you." She gives me a soft smile, and I wish I could scoop her up and take her home with me.

"Is there anything else you can think of that we need from the store?"

"No. I can stop after work. I don't mind."

"Nope. You come straight home to me." I lean in and kiss her cheek again. "I'll see you soon, baby. Enjoy the rest of your day." I turn to leave, waving at the receptionist on my way out.

The grocery store wasn't as busy as I expected it to be, but I was still there for over an hour. I went up and down every aisle, grabbing snacks I've seen Brogan buy since we've been together. Basically, I bought way too much food, but that time of the month is here, and I don't know what she's in the mood for. Not that I won't go back out and grab her whatever she wants or needs, but I wanted her to be stocked, just in case. I also grabbed her favorite ice cream, thanks to a quick text to her sister, as well as some chocolate bars.

I was thinking ahead and took pictures on my phone of all of her feminine products, so finding those and tossing two boxes of each into the cart was a breeze. I don't know how many she needs, but I figured two boxes of each were a safe bet.

My phone rings as I'm wrapping up, putting everything away. "Hello?" I answer, not looking at the screen as I take the trash out to the can in the garage.

"What are you doing today?" Lachlan asks.

"I just got back from the store, and I'm getting ready to dust and make dinner."

"Ugh, I hate dusting," he complains.

"I don't know anyone who enjoys it, but it has to be done."

"Yeah," he says, and I can almost guarantee he's looking around his house and seeing that he needs to dust. "Where's the wife today?"

"She had to work."

"Bummer. All right, well, I'm heading to my parents' for the night. My mom keeps saying I never come to see her, and the guilt is heavy, so we're having dinner, and I'll chill there for a while. I was going to invite you to come along, but I'm pretty sure I know what your answer will be." He chuckles.

"Yeah, I plan to have dinner ready and the house in order when Brogan gets home, so she'll sit and relax after working all day." I don't tell him that it's that time of the month for her, and I plan to pamper her. That's information for me and my wife only. "Tell them I said hello."

"Will do. Kiss Brogan for me."

"Over my dead body," I clip, and the fucker laughs in my ear as he hangs up. "Asshole," I mutter, but I'm smiling. Lachlan knew exactly what he was doing, and that it would get me riled up. Just wait. One day it's going to be him, and I'm taking notes. I'll be repaying him the favor tenfold.

I crank up the radio and get to work dusting the house. That leads me to cleaning the bathroom, and before I know it, it's time to start dinner. Brogan mentioned a few nights ago that meatloaf sounded good, so thanks to my mom, who is still annoyed with me that she has not met my new wife, and that I got married without telling her, I have her recipe, and I'm ready to get to work. I just hope I don't fuck this up.

I promised my parents that we would come to their place for dinner soon. I'm going to talk to Brogan tonight so we can set something up. I'm stoked for them to meet her, and I know without a doubt they're going to fall for her, just as I am.

It's a little after five when I hear the front door open. I'm in the kitchen pulling the meatloaf from the oven when Brogan walks into the kitchen.

"Something smells good," she says.

"I made my mom's famous meatloaf."

"You made meatloaf?"

"Yeah, you said it's been sounding good to you. I also made mashed potatoes, but from a box, and mac and cheese."

"Thank you for this. What can I do to help?" she asks, taking off her coat and hanging it on the back of the chair at the island.

"Nothing. I'm all set here. I'll make us each a plate. I have the table set and two glasses of tea ready to go unless you want something else?"

"No. Tea is great. Thank you, Maddox." She comes over and places her hand on my arm as I'm cutting up the meatloaf. "This is really sweet of you."

Leaning over, I press a kiss to the corner of her mouth. "I wanted you to be able to come home and relax. The grocery shopping is done, and I picked up some of your favorites. I know women get cravings, and I hope I hit them all, but if not, I'll gladly go pick up anything you need or want."

"Maddox." Her face turns that adorable shade of pink that I love on her.

"I'm your husband, Brogan. We're partners in this life, and I'm here for you, even for snacks, tampons, or whatever else you need. Never be afraid to ask or talk to me about this stuff."

"Are all men this open?" she asks.

"I know my four best friends are, and as for me, I'm just me. What you see is what you get, and you get all of me. One day, I hope I'll have all of you too." I turn back to dishing up our plates, and then to carry them to the dining room to find her still standing there watching me.

"You're spoiling me."

"Good." I nod toward the dining room. "Let's eat." Once we're sitting at the table, and we've started to eat, I ask, "How was your day?"

"Good. My husband surprised me with my favorite drink, and the day flew by after that."

I almost choke on my bite of meatloaf, and not because it sucks—it's fucking delicious. No, it's because she referred to me as her husband. Fucking finally, I feel like we're making progress. In the past month we've lived together, I fall a little more for her every day.

"I'm glad." I wink at her, and she giggles, and just like that, she steals another piece of my heart. We talk while we eat and it's the perfect dinner at home, just the two of us.

"I'll clean up," I tell her once we're finished. "Go take a hot bath or shower or whatever, and you and I have a date with a rom-com and all the snacks you can eat. I even have the heating pad on the couch. I found it in the bathroom when I was cleaning."

"Maddox, really?" she asks, smiling and blushing at the same time.

"I can't pretend to know how it feels, but I have a mother, and grew up with Forrest pretty much raising Emerson, so I know it can be hell."

"Is all of this in the *How to Make My Wife Melt into a Puddle* handbook?" she asks.

"No, this is the 'I don't know what the hell I'm doing, but I want to be there for you,' Maddox edition." I tap my temple. "Go on. I'll clean up and meet you in the living room."

"Thank you for this, for dinner, and… everything."

"You're welcome, baby." She turns to leave, and I quickly clean up dinner and pack away the leftovers. Thirty minutes later, she steps into the living room to find me lying on the couch. I pat the spot in front of me, and she barely hesitates before she lies down. I wrap the blanket around her and pull her to my chest. "You need the heating pad?" I ask her.

"No, I'm okay."

"Here." I hand her the remote. "Pick something."

"What are you in the mood for?"

"We could be watching paint dry, and I'd be thrilled because you're in my arms, Brogan."

She chuckles. "Okay, well, how about this new series?" She motions to the screen. "Briar mentioned that she and Forrest started it and it's really good."

"Perfect."

She starts the show, and I snuggle her closer. I move my hand to her belly and slowly creep my hand under her shirt, and rub soothing circles on her abdomen. At least I hope they're soothing. Honestly, I'm out of my depth here, but she's not stopping me, so it must not be hurting her even if it's not helping.

We watch two episodes when she has to get up to use the restroom. "Do you want a snack?" I ask her.

"What are my options?" I rattle off everything I bought for her today and her eyes grow wide. "You bought all of my favorites."

"I know." I grin.

"How about some cherry cordial ice cream?"

"You got it." I climb off the couch, out of my comfortable cocoon, and make us both a big bowl, and I'm ready for her when she gets back.

"Thank you," she says, sitting right next to me on the couch, and covering both of our legs with the blanket.

"So, my parents want to meet you." I feel bad putting them off as long as I have, but if she's not ready, they're just going to have to keep waiting. These aren't normal circumstances, and I want her to be ready.

She nods. "I was wondering when this conversation was going to happen."

"They've been patiently waiting, according to my mom." I laugh.

"When?"

"Whenever you feel up to it."

"Next weekend?"

I try hard to hide my surprise. She's in this. She might not be able to admit it out loud, but she wants this to work between us as much as I do. I can feel it. "Sure, Mom wants to make us dinner, so I'll tell her to choose a day, and we'll go from there."

"Okay."

"Thank you." The sincerity of my tone is evident. This means the world to me. I hate that I didn't get to meet her father, but I'd like to think he would approve of me, of us. How could he not? I adore his daughter.

She tilts her head to the side to study me. "Together."

I'm sure my smile is blinding. "Together." We finish our ice cream in silence, but we keep sharing these looks. Ones that have hope growing inside me. We're going to do this. I know the woman sitting next to me is my future. I can see it, and every day that I spend with her, she takes another little piece of me to call her own.

"Another episode?" she asks as she takes my empty bowl with hers, and places them on the end table.

"Definitely." She stands and nods for me to lie down, and not one to pass up an opportunity to have her in my arms, I do and wait for her to take her spot in front of me. Again, I wrap the blanket around us and snuggle her close.

I couldn't tell you a single thing that happened in this episode because all I see is her. My wife, who is lying in my arms. My wife, who I'll go to sleep holding just as I am now.

"Did you dust?" she asks. She can't see my grin, but I love that I was able to surprise her and take some of her burden. Besides, I live here too. Cleaning shouldn't fall just to her.

"I did."

"You took care of everything on my list."

"Yep." Pride swells in my chest. I took care of her list, because I'm taking care of her. That's all I want.

"You didn't have to do that."

"But then I wouldn't be able to do this." I kiss her cheek. "I was missing you today anyway, so it kept me busy."

She pauses, then glances at me over her shoulder. "You missed me today?"

"Yes."

"How am I supposed to resist you, Maddox Lanigan?"

"You're not."

"I was certain this entire situation would be a disaster, and now…"

"What about now?" I ask her when she remains quiet.

"Now, it's the complete opposite."

I hug her a little tighter. "I know that took a lot for you to say, and we're still just taking it one day at a time, but I can tell you that if I had to choose between a night out with the guys, and a night in like this with you, that a night in with you wins hands down every single time. I'm falling hard for you, Mrs. Lanigan."

She rolls over to face me. "Ditto, Mr. Lanigan."

I cup her jaw and stare into her big green eyes. I see what she's not willing to say. She's afraid to hope, but that's okay, because I have enough for both of us. "Can I kiss you?" She's so close, and I want nothing more than to show her how I feel about her. I've been telling her that I want her, but something inside me screams to also show her.

"I might be bad at it."

"Impossible." No fucking way is this woman bad at anything. Not in my eyes.

"I don't know... my experience is pretty much nil unless you count some sloppy tries during my senior year of high school. I don't have much faith."

"Let me prove you wrong." Leaning in, I hover, giving her a chance to stop me, but she doesn't take it. I close the remaining distance and capture her lips with mine. Just a light brush, and when she doesn't pull away, I nip at her bottom lip. She gasps, and I take the opening for what it is and slide my tongue against hers. She mimics my actions and melts into me as we get lost in one another.

She whimpers, and I take that as a sign to keep going as I slide my tongue against hers. Her hands find their way to my shirt, and she grips it tightly. She's pulling me closer, not pushing me away, and my cock throbs at the thought.

My wife wants me.

That's all I need to know to allow my hands to roam. They find their way to the curve of her ass, as I squeeze, and she moans. Lifting her leg, I toss it over mine. My cock is now nestled between her thighs, but that's as far as I take it. I have her here, in my arms, and that's enough for now. She told me this was pretty much her first real kiss; at least, that's what I chose to hear.

This kiss is the only one that matters.

I can't help but think about our wedding night. Surely, we kissed to seal our fate. I wish more than anything I could remember that night. The night she became mine.

When we finally come up for air, I rest my forehead against hers. I take a few moments to catch my breath, and from how her chest rises and falls, she needs the time to do the same.

"What about now?" I ask, my voice raspy and laced with desire. It's all for her.

"That didn't suck." She has this dazed look in her eyes as she offers me a shy smile.

"Yeah?" I chuckle. "Should we try it again?"

"I think I need something to compare it to."

That's how I spend the rest of the night, kissing my wife like we're teenagers. Something she never got to experience, and something I'm thrilled she gets to do with me, and only me.

BROGAN 9

MADDOX HAS MY HAND IN his firm yet gentle grip as we make our way to the front door of his parents' house. It's been a week today since I agreed to dinner, and as we take the last step, I'm wondering what in the hell I was thinking. Oh wait, my sexy husband was asking me to meet his family, and I couldn't tell him no. I promised to give this a shot, and I have been, but meeting the parents, that's new for me. Another first that will belong to Maddox.

"Breathe, baby." Maddox bends to whisper in my ear. "They're going to love you. I promise you, everything is going to be okay."

"I've never had to do this, Maddox. And you're their son who goes on a trip and comes back with a wife they've never met."

"Trust me, beautiful. If at any time you feel uncomfortable, we'll leave. Just tap your cheek with your index finger, and I'll make an excuse for us to go."

"I can't do that. This is your family. I'll be okay." I square my shoulders and hope like hell my words are true.

"Brogan Lanigan, you are my wife. You are my family and my priority. If you're not comfortable, then we leave. You don't know them yet, but believe me when I tell you if it were my mom who was uncomfortable, my dad would be getting her the hell out of there." He kisses my temple. "You'll see."

With one hand still gripping mine, he pushes open the front door. "We're here!" he calls out.

"Finally!" a female voice calls back. I hear feet moving down the hall, and a woman appears with a tall man who looks like an older version of Maddox standing behind her, wearing a kind smile. "Oh, she's beautiful." She bypasses Maddox and comes for me, wrapping me in a hug.

A swarm of emotions hit me with her embrace. Sadness that I missed these types of hugs with my mother. Longing as I wish she were here, and relief that his mother is so accepting of me, a stranger her son married, and she's welcoming me into their lives.

I grip Maddox's hand, and he chuckles. "Mom, take it easy, yeah?"

"Maddox Lanigan, you've made me wait almost thirty-four years for a daughter. I will not take it easy." She gives him a glare that would bring a lesser man to his knees before turning back to me, and a smile transforms her face. "I'm Cassie. You can call me Cassie or Mom, whichever you prefer, and this is Hank."

"Let me have my turn, sweetheart," Hank says, chuckling. Cassie harrumphs but steps aside and allows Hank room to bend down and wrap me in a hug. "Welcome to the family. Hank or Dad is fine."

"It's nice to meet you," I tell them. My voice cracks from the overwhelming emotions coursing through me.

"Mom, Dad, this is my wife, Brogan. Wife, these are my parents, Cassie and Hank Lanigan."

"Come in, come in." Cassie moves to stand next to me and loops her arm through mine. "My son has been greedy, so it's my turn. I hope you like lasagna," she says, leading me down the hall.

"Mom, she's mine!" Maddox calls back, and I can hear the humor in his voice.

"Maddox, I taught you how to share."

"Not my wife."

"Let her have this, son." I hear his dad say.

"If she makes Brogan uncomfortable, we're out of here," Maddox replies.

Although I'm embarrassed to have all the attention on me, I'm also grateful for the man I married and his willingness to put me first. My dad was the first and last man to ever do that, and I allowed myself to forget how that felt until this moment.

"Oh, he's smitten. Good job," Cassie whispers in my ear, laughing as we enter the kitchen. "Tell me everything," Cassie says, pointing to a barstool at the counter. "My son tells me nothing."

I feel strong hands grip my shoulders, and the heat of him against my back. "She's not yours," Maddox says, teasing his mother. Their banter, and the kind smiles of both of his parents, help put me at ease.

"Oh, my dear boy, you're delusional. I don't care what you say. You're sharing her with me." Cassie turns her eyes back to me. "I've lived with all this testosterone for far too long. I needed another woman in this house. These two"—she points to Maddox and Hank—"finally have some competition." She leans over the counter and holds her hand up for a high-five, and I chuckle as I slap my hand against hers. "You boys are in for it," she says, a glimmer of humor dancing in her eyes.

"Bring it, baby," Hank says. He moves behind her, places his hands on her hips, and kisses her cheek.

"Told you," Maddox says, his lips next to my ear.

I glance at him over my shoulder. "They're great." I mean that with everything that I am. My heart is smiling at the obvious love this family shares for one another. It makes me miss my dad, but it also makes me grateful for the man standing next to me. For what he's brought into my life. I swallow back the lump in my throat and focus on the here and now.

He leans forward and kisses the tip of my nose. "So are you."

It's hard for me to believe this moment is real. I want to pinch myself to make sure this isn't a dream. I feel too comfortable, too safe for it not to be, but when I covertly pinch the side of my thigh, and it smarts, I know this is real. This is my new life, if I have the courage to take it. If I find it in myself to dig deep and leave the past behind, and live for the future. Could the walls that hold so many pictures of the lives of the Maddox's family one day include me? Could this be my new family?

My heart tells me yes, and I want so badly to believe it.

"Maddox, stop hogging her. Brogan, tell me about you," Cassie says.

"Well, I'm a twin."

"A twin. Hank, did you hear that? Maybe we'll have twin grandbabies," she says, smiling widely.

I can't help but laugh at her enthusiasm. I feel my body relax. Maddox's hands move back to my shoulders, and his touch is the comfort I need, or maybe it's just him. Shaking out of my thoughts, I reply, "My twin sister, Briar, has twin four-year-old daughters."

"Oh, that's right. She married our Forrest."

"She did." I smile.

"He's smitten, from what I hear," Cassie replies.

"He definitely is. Those three ladies have him wrapped around their fingers," Maddox tells her.

"They really do." I smile, thinking about how happy Forrest has made my sister and my nieces.

"Wouldn't that be great? Three sets of twins in the family?" Cassie asks Hank.

"Sure would," he replies, smiling at her as if his entire universe revolves around her.

"You have other twins in the family? Maddox hadn't mentioned that."

"You and Briar, and your nieces, that's two. If you and Maddox have twins, that would be three."

"Y-You're counting us?" I ask in disbelief.

"Of course we are. You're family. And Forrest has been one of our extra sons since the boys were little. We'd include his wife and daughters regardless, but they're also your sister and nieces, so that's just an added bonus."

I swallow hard. I don't know what to say to that. My heart feels heavy, not because of her words or simple acceptance, but because I'm missing my parents. My mom, I don't remember her, but my dad used to talk about her all the time. My dad would have loved Forrest and Maddox both, and there isn't a doubt in my mind that he would also include them, all of them, as members of our family.

"Thank you," I whisper. I feel Maddox's arms come around me in a tight hug.

"I didn't mean to upset you. I know I'm a lot, just ask Hank," Cassie says softly. "I just want you to know this is your family now, all of you."

I nod and clear my throat.

"You want to go?" Maddox asks. His voice is soft, just for me.

I shake my head. "Dinner smells delicious," I say, trying to move past my sadness of missing my parents.

"Thank you. It's ready. Everyone make a plate, and we'll eat in the dining room."

It's a flurry of activity while we make our plates, gather drinks, and head to the dining room. Dinner is delicious, and the company is perfect. I was so nervous to be here tonight, but just like their son, Cassie and Hank Lanigan make me feel as if I've always been a part of their world.

I stare at the pictures on the walls, and I want more than anything to be included in this family's history. Maybe, just maybe, babies of my own, and I wouldn't be mad if it was the third set of twins as Cassie said. It's all too much, too overwhelming, and it scares the hell out of me, the more I want for it to be my future.

<hr />

"We need to have a girls' day," Cassie says as we put on our coats to head home.

"I'd really love that."

"Your sister should come too." I can see it in her eyes what she's not saying. Over dinner, I shared that both of my parents have passed, and Cassie wants to be there for us. That's just the person she is, and I'm grateful for her easy acceptance.

There's a small part of me that worries that getting closer to them could cause more heartache if this thing between Maddox and me doesn't work out. I know I'm not supposed to think that way, but it's hard not to worry. That's just who I am. Life has taught me that nothing ever stays the same.

"I'm sure she would be thrilled to go," I tell her honestly. "Thank you for dinner."

"Any time. You two be safe." Cassie pulls me into a hug, then does the same with Maddox before stepping back and letting Hank have his turn.

Maddox laces his fingers with mine and we leave their home the same way we entered. Tethered together. Maddox opens my door for me and waits for me to settle before closing the door behind me. When he slides into his seat behind the wheel, he reaches over and takes my hand in his, bringing it to his lips.

"How was it?"

"Perfect. They're incredible, Maddox."

"They loved you. I think my mom is ready to trade me in for you." He laughs.

"Never." I giggle. I feel... lighter somehow. I needed tonight and didn't even realize it. Somehow, I think my husband did. He seems to always know what I need. He knew his parents would welcome me. It was my fear that was eating at me, but it was unwarranted. His parents are amazing.

"I love that." He's got this dopey smile on his face, and it makes me want to know every single thing about him. It makes me want to kiss him, but I stay in my seat, on my side of the truck.

"What?" I ask.

"The sound of your laugh." Another kiss to the back of my hand, and he places our joined hands on his thigh as he backs out of the driveway.

"I'm sorry about your mom. Your dad too," he adds.

"Thank you. I don't remember my mom, but my dad talked about her all the time. He made sure she was a part of our lives." I don't have any memories of my mother that are my own. My dad made sure he talked about her often, so even though I don't remember her, I feel like I know her. I feel her loss, and my love for her—this person who helped create me and my sister that I don't remember—is so strong that I still miss her, miss them both every single day.

"He sounds like a great man."

"He was." I turn and stare out the window. "He would have loved you and Forrest both." He gives my hand a gentle squeeze. "He would have given you both a hard time, but he would have loved you." I pause and decide to just say what I'm thinking. I make a mental note to tell Susan. She's going to be so proud. "You're a lot like him. Kind, caring, gentle—all the things that made him a great man." My voice cracks because I miss him. I miss him so fucking much. I'm feeling it more since Briar and the girls moved out. The last month with Maddox has filled the lonely nights, but the sadness of our father not meeting the men in our lives is soul-crushing at times.

I can't help but wonder for the first time what my dad would think about the situation I've found myself in. I don't have to think long. His first question would have been if he treats me well. The answer of course is a resounding yes, and the second, would have been if I'm happy. A month ago, I might not have been able to answer that one, but tonight, I can confidently say yes, and that scares the hell out of me for what's yet to come.

Maddox pulls the truck over to the side of the road. We're halfway home, but there are nothing but houses on this road, and as far as I know, it's none of the guys'. "What are we doing?" I ask him.

He puts the truck in Park and opens his door. My eyes follow him as he stalks around the front of the truck, the headlights lighting his way. He pulls open my door and stares at me for a few seconds.

"It's cold as hell out here, so I'm going to need you to lift up and make room." He taps my thigh, but I'm still trying to process what he wants.

"What?" I choke out. "What are you doing?" I question him.

"I need to hold you, Brogan. I just need to, so lift that perfect ass up and make room for me. It's cold out here, and I don't want you to freeze because I'm needy."

With my heart in my throat, I do as he asks, unbuckle my seat belt, and stand as best as I can. He slides in, pulling me onto his lap, before closing the door. He wraps his arms around me and buries his face in my neck. "I wish I could have met him. Both of them. I could show him what you mean to me. I'd like to think that he could see it, but I'd tell him that his daughter changed my life and that his daughter is the best thing that ever happened to me. You, Brogan, my dear wife, are the best thing that's ever happened to me." His voice is raspy with emotion, and his words, they wrap themselves around my heart.

I can't explain it, but this moment feels right. I know I'm exactly where I'm meant to be—cradled in the comfort of his arms. I bite down on my bottom lip to keep from crying. All I can do is relax into him and place my hands over his where they are banded around my waist. There is so much I want to say. That if my dad were here, he'd tell me to turn my busy brain off and follow my heart. I want to tell him that every day he captures another piece of me that I was never going to allow someone else to take, but this man, with his strong determination and his kind heart, is collecting pieces one day at a time.

I don't know how long we sit here on the side of the road, in front of a random house, but I know that once again, my husband knew what I needed. I needed to feel his arms around me. I needed his hot breath against my skin. I just needed him, and to my surprise, it's not as scary as it was a month ago.

"I need to get you home." He places his lips against my neck. It's a tender press of his lips and sends shivers down my spine. "Are you cold, baby?"

"No." I'm quick to answer, and my husband is a smart man. He kisses me again in the same spot, knowing the effect he has on me. I lift up, and he opens the door and slides out. Reaching in, he pulls my seat belt across me and fastens it before closing the door and jogging back to his side of the truck.

The rest of the ride home is quiet, but not uncomfortable. It's quite the opposite. I feel seen. I feel safe and cared for. All things I've only received from my sister and nieces since losing our dad.

Maddox gave me that. He's given me that every single day since we woke up in that hotel together in Vegas with rings on our fingers.

"Are we watching some TV or are we going to bed?" Maddox questions as we walk into the house.

"Can we watch TV in bed?" I ask.

"We can. Do you need anything from the kitchen?" he inquires as he takes my coat and hangs it next to his on the hook.

"I don't think so," I say, kicking off my shoes to leave them to drip dry on the rug by the door. Maddox does the same.

"Great." He bends and lifts me over his shoulder, and I shriek with laughter.

"What are you doing?" I smack his ass.

"That won't entice me to put you down, wife. You should know by now that I love it when your hands are on me."

"Maddox!" I cackle with laughter.

He carries me into the bedroom, dropping me on the mattress with a bounce, before turning on the bedside lamp. "There she is," he says quietly. He bends over, bracing his body with one hand on the bed while the other cradles my cheek. "I love that smile." He leans in and kisses me.

One more kiss and he's standing back to his full height. "You want the bathroom first?" he asks.

I'm breathless, just as I am after every touch of his lips to mine. Something tells me that I'll never get used to the affection this man gives so freely. "No. You go ahead."

He winks and grabs clothes to change into before disappearing into the bathroom. I sit up on the bed and plug in my phone to charge. When he opens the bathroom door, he tosses a shirt at me.

"What's this?"

"My shirt."

"And why are you tossing it at my head?" I ask, pulling the shirt to my chest. I can smell him, and it takes extreme effort not to bring it to my face to sniff it, but I know he's watching me.

"I thought you might want to sleep in it." He shrugs.

My heart gallops in my chest. I always sleep in pajamas that keep my top and bottom half covered, at least I have since Maddox moved in. I want more with him. I want to know what it's like to have his hands roam over my body, and if I'm being honest, there's a giddiness inside me thinking about sleeping in his shirt.

I feel like a teenager, and I hear Susan's voice in my head telling me to allow myself to feel what I feel, and experience the parts of life that I missed out on. So, I stand and offer my husband a smile.

"Thank you." I don't stick around to see the look on his face, but I can imagine he's smiling just as I am as I slip into the bathroom and close the door behind me. I lift the shirt to my face and sniff. His masculine woodsy scent invades my senses and my entire body lights up.

I quickly change and go through my nightly routine, and before I can second-guess myself, I flip off the light and open the door. Maddox is in bed, his back resting against pillows that are stacked up against the headboard.

"Fuck."

I bite the inside of my cheek to keep from smiling. I take slow, steady steps toward the bed, and he lifts the covers, inviting me in.

"Come on over here, Brogan."

I grin, but do as he asks, and settle into his side, resting my head against his bare chest. "What are we watching?"

He huffs out a laugh. "Do you really think I can focus on anything but you right now?"

I lift my head to peer up at him. "Do you want me to go change?"

"No." He wraps his arms a little tighter around me. Keeping me close. "No, I don't want you to change."

"So, no movie. I guess we could talk."

"Talk," he chokes out. "Yeah, we can do that."

I start to move away and his arms tighten again. "I'm going to turn out the light." He reluctantly lets me go as I slide across the mattress to turn off the lamp and move back to the middle of the bed. He's now lying on his side, so I do the same facing him. We have nothing but the moonlight filtering into the room, but I can still make out his features.

"Do you want kids?" he asks.

"Starting with the heavy hitters, huh?" I tease.

"Blame my mom."

I chuckle softly, before taking a deep breath and answering him honestly. "I never thought I'd find a man I could trust enough to be vulnerable with to get to that point. However, I love kids, and I'd love to be a mom. Watching Briar with the girls—yes. One day. What about you?"

"With my wife, yeah, I want to be a dad."

"You don't have to be married these days," I say, a little defensively.

"Hey." His hand reaches up and smooths my hair back out of my eyes. "You misunderstood me. I said with my wife. *You* are my wife, Brogan."

"Oh." I did take his answer wrong, and I'm floored by his reply.

"How many?" he asks, saving me from floundering in his response.

"A couple, at least."

"The chance of twins is high. Would you want that?"

"Yeah." I smile. "I loved growing up with my best friend. River and Rayne remind me so much of Briar and me when we were growing up. What about you?"

"At least two. It was lonely being an only child. Well, kind of. I had the guys, and we all spent a lot of time together."

"At least two," I repeat.

"At least two. With my wife." He moves closer, and our bodies are now aligned. He rests his hand on my bare hip, and I suck in a breath. "You set the pace, Brogan. You decide what happens between us."

My insecurities start to rear their ugly head, but somehow, he knows and soothes me.

"Stop that. All I see is you. You're the only woman I've seen for far too long. You're perfect." He slides his hand up my bare back in a feather-soft touch.

I shiver at the contact. "I like it when you touch me," I whisper, not sure he can hear me over the rapid beat of my heart.

"Your skin is so soft." His hand continues to stroke gently up and down my spine. He ventures to my belly, and slowly, his hand creeps up. "Is this okay?"

I swallow past the lump in my throat. "Y-Yes."

"Touch me," he murmurs. "There isn't a single thing you could do to me that I won't like."

"I don't know how." I close my eyes, my confession hanging between us.

"There is no right or wrong answer here, Brogan. I'm yours to explore."

I want that. I want that so much. My hand trembles as I place it on his bare chest and tentatively move over his abs. "Hard, yet smooth," I blurt.

He hums and moves his hand higher. His thumb traces over my nipple, and I can't stop the moan that falls from my lips. That doesn't stop him as he explores my body with a soft, gentle touch.

I do the same, reaching the waistband of his boxer briefs, and my hand stills. "Sorry," I mutter.

"Don't. Everything I am is yours, Brogan Lanigan."

"I've never...." My voice trails off.

"Good. It makes me really fucking happy that I'm the only man you're going to touch like this."

"The only?" I ask.

"You heard me, baby. I know that makes me an asshole because I've... been here before, but I need you to know no moments before this one matter. They're all forgotten. There is no one but you."

His words make me feel brave. So, with a trembling hand, I slide my hand beneath the waistband of his underwear and I feel him—hard and like silk—as I palm his stiff length.

"Shit," he hisses.

"Am I hurting you?" I release him.

"Don't you fucking dare," he grounds out. "You're not hurting me. It feels so damn good to have your hands on me."

"I was just touching you," I say, not sure how good that could actually feel.

He moves his fingers back under my shirt and palms my breast, and I moan. "See," he says smugly.

"Yeah," I agree. "I don't know what to do."

"Tonight, we explore. We get to know one another by touch, but that's it. Our hands can roam, but that's where it ends. Are you okay with that?"

"I'm okay with that." I'm more than okay with that. He always knows what I need. His unwavering understanding and guidance are a turn-on, but I'll never tell him that. Knowing I can say no, or admit that I'm inexperienced or scared gives me the confidence I need to keep going. To let my hands explore him.

Slowly, I slide my hand back beneath his waistband, and grip his cock. "Tell me what to do," I murmur.

"Touch me. That's all tonight is about. Touching and exploring."

I'm nervous, but I do as he says. I stroke his hard length, getting a feel for the weight of him in the palm of my hand. It's much... softer than I thought it would be.

He huffs out a laugh. "Good to know."

"I said that out loud, didn't I?" I ask, mortified.

"You did, but that's okay, because your skin feels like silk." He palms my breast, his thumb tracing over my hard nipple, and pleasure rolls through me. So much so that I can't hide it when my body shudders.

He stays there for a while, and I continue to gently stroke him. I have no idea what I'm doing, but he doesn't seem to mind, and I like touching him, so I don't stop. Maddox slides his hand up the back of my shirt and traces my spine.

Removing my hand from his boxer briefs, I let it trail over his abs, and to his face. The scruff of today's beard tickles the palm of my hand, but I like it. My hand moves to the back of his neck, and over his short hair, before mimicking his movements and tracing along his spine.

We take our time touching and learning each other's bodies. When he slides his big hands beneath the waistband of my panties and cups my ass, I bite my cheek to keep from moaning. However, when he moves his hand to the front and traces his index finger through my folds, I can't stop it.

"That's... nice," I confess. My face flames, because that's the least sexy thing I could say, but I'm nervous and so turned on right now I can't seem to think straight.

"When you're ready," he tells me, "I can show you how nice. This is just the beginning."

"You'll teach me?" I ask as he runs his finger through my folds a second time.

"We'll learn together," he mutters.

"Maddox, you don't have to pretend. I know this isn't... new for you."

"You're wrong." He removes his hand and brings it to his lips, and with the glow of the moonlight I watch as he sucks his finger into his mouth. He closes his eyes and moans, and I have to rub my thighs together to ward off the desire that simple act causes inside me. "You are the first woman I've cared about this much, Brogan. Everything with you is new and exciting. So, yes, baby, we will learn together."

I don't know what to say to that, so instead, I keep touching him. Everywhere my hands can reach, I touch. His do the same. I lose all track of time. As we explore each other's bodies, but just by touch. It's sensual and erotic, and I've never been this turned on in my life, but he holds strong on his decision that nothing else is happening tonight.

When I can barely keep my eyes open, he kisses me softly. "Goodnight, sweet Brogan."

"Night," I mumble, and fall asleep in his arms, which is quickly becoming my favorite place to be.

MADDOX 10

FOR THE FIRST TIME IN my life, I want to celebrate Valentine's Day. I've dotted all my i's and crossed all my t's. I've planned the perfect date for me and my wife. We're having dinner at one of her favorite restaurants. I was lucky I was able to get last-minute reservations because I didn't find out until dinner at my parents' house last week when she was talking to my mom that Mario's Italian restaurant in Nashville was one of her favorites. Her dad used to take Briar and Brogan there when they were celebrating, and tonight, we have something to celebrate.

Us.

She has no idea where we are going, only that we're going out and how to dress. "Brogan!" I call out to her. "I'm going to run uptown and fill the truck up. I'll be back in less than twenty," I tell her.

She sticks her head out of the bedroom door. "We can just stop on the way to save you a trip."

"Nah, it's fine. I don't mind." I walk toward her because when my wife is near, I have to be close to her. It's an addiction that she's thankfully supporting. I bend and kiss her lips. "I'll be right back."

"Okay, silly man." She shakes her head and disappears back into the bedroom to finish getting ready.

After rushing out of the house, I head to town. Not to get gas, I did that last night on my way home from the shop. I make it to the florist just as they close to pick up the bouquet of red roses I ordered.

When I get back to the house, I ring the doorbell instead of going inside. When Brogan answers, she looks confused but so fucking beautiful. She's wearing a black dress that hugs her curves, and her hair hangs in loose curls down her back.

"You're beautiful," I tell her.

She blushes. "Thank you. What are you doing ringing the doorbell? Did you forget your key?"

"I'm picking my girl up for a date." I watch as my words sink in, and her eyes soften.

"Maddox." She places her hand over her heart and her eyes shimmer with tears.

"These are for you." I hand her the flowers and peck her cheek with a kiss. "Happy Valentine's Day."

"They're beautiful." She smiles up at me. "Happy Valentine's Day," she says shyly.

"They don't compare to you."

"I've already agreed to dinner," she teases.

"Another first," I tell her, and her smile lights up the entire fucking sky.

"Come on in and I'll put this inside." She stares down at the vase, because I remembered from last time.

She carries the flowers to the kitchen and places them on the island. I stand back and watch as she pulls out her phone and takes a couple of pictures before turning to face me.

"You ready?"

"I am. Still no hints as to where we're going?" she asks.

"My lips are sealed. I can tell you we're headed to Nashville."

"Nashville. The possibilities are endless."

"Exactly." I help her into her coat before offering her my arm. She takes it without hesitation and leans into me as I walk her out to my truck. "My lady," I say, opening the door for her.

"Thank you, Mad," she whispers.

I nod and rush around to my side of the truck. "That scarf is pretty. It brings out your eyes," I tell her.

"Thank you. I, um, I actually made it."

"What? You made that?" I ask, taking another quick glance at her, before turning my eyes back onto the road.

"Yeah, I used to crochet a lot. I know it's nerdy, but it's relaxing for me. I got back into it pretty heavily when Briar and the girls moved out. It helped pass the loneliness."

"I've not seen you do it."

"It's been a while, well, since you moved in, actually."

"Why? If it's something that you enjoy?"

"I don't know. I guess I didn't want to show you the nerdy me."

"Brogan, I want every piece of you." I reach over and rest my hand on her thigh. "There isn't a single hobby you could have that would make me not want to be right next to you while you do it."

"Right." She laughs. "Like you want to sit beside me while I crochet each night?" She says it like the thought is preposterous, when in reality, we could be staring at the blank wall, and I'd be thrilled to be next to her. That's how far I've fallen for my wife.

"Why not? You enjoy it. Of course I'd want to watch you do something you love. Maybe I can even convince you to make me something."

"You don't have to say that."

"I mean it. It's cold as hell this time of year." She's quiet for several minutes.

"What kind of wife would I be if I didn't make something for my husband?"

My heart hammers in my chest and I swallow hard. Fuck me, does she understand what it does to me when she refers to me as her husband? "Mine," I tell her. "You'd be mine, and no pressure," I answer.

"I'll see what I can do."

"Thank you."

"You haven't even seen it yet," she says, and I can hear the humor in her tone.

"I've seen yours. I know you're incredible. It's going to be great."

"What about you? Any secret hobbies I don't know about?"

"Nah, I like to draw. Hence the job, but other than that, just hanging out with the guys. We used to go fishing a lot when we were younger, but once we were old enough to drink, we'd just chill at someone's house, usually Forrest's because he would have Emerson."

"I've never had a lot of friends. I had Briar, and that was enough for me. However, I can admit it's nice to have Emerson, Monroe, and Maggie added to that list."

"And me. Did I make the list?"

"Are you my friend?" she asks, teasing.

"If by friend you mean I get to kiss the air from your lungs and touch every inch of your sexy body, then, yeah, beautiful, we're the best of friends."

Her laughter fills the cab of my truck, and I wish I could record the sound to play for times when she's not with me.

"Mario's. We're going to Mario's," she says, as I pull my truck into the lot.

"Your favorite, right?"

She nods, tears welling in her eyes. "The last time I was here was our high school graduation. Right before our dad was diagnosed with cancer."

"We can go somewhere else." Fuck, I didn't think about this place bringing up painful memories for her.

"No. Please, no. I want to be here." She takes off her seat belt and turns to face me. "I don't know how you always know what I need, Maddox Lanigan, but this, it's perfect. This was our special place, and now I get to share it with you."

Pride swells in my chest that I get to share a good memory of her past with her. Maybe we'll make this a tradition with our kids, a special place to go when we celebrate. We can tell them it's where their grandpa used to take their mom, and where we went on our first date. I know I'm getting ahead of myself, but I can see it. "He would be proud of you and the woman you've become."

She blinks her tears away, and fans at her face with her hands. "Don't make me cry before we go in there." She smiles. "This is perfect, Maddox. Thank you."

"You're welcome. Now, stay put. I'll get your door."

"I'd expect nothing less from the man I married." She gives me a watery smile, and I feel that smile in my chest. It fists my heart, gripping tightly, refusing to let go. Not that I want it to.

I rush around the truck, open her door for her, then lead her into the restaurant with my hand on the small of her back. When we reach the hostess, Brogan speaks for us, which surprises me.

"Reservation for Lanigan."

I squeeze her hip because fuck, each day she accepts this, us, a little more, and my hope builds. We're building a life together. We're working on forever.

"Tonight was amazing," Brogan says, as we're making our way to the bedroom. "I'd forgotten how much I love their food."

"It was the first time for me, but we will definitely be going back. Maybe we can take Briar, Forrest, and the girls with us next time?" I suggest.

She turns to look at me, hope in her big green eyes. "I'd love that, Maddox."

"You ready for bed?"

"Yes. My belly is full, and I could crash."

"Need a lift?" I ask her.

She grins. "I think I can manage." She steps closer, stands on her tiptoes, and kisses me. "Thank you for the best Valentine's Day and first date a girl could ask for."

"First date?"

"As an adult. Prom doesn't count."

"Only our time together counts." I nod.

"Come on. Let's go to bed." She holds her hand out for me, and I take it, allowing her to lead us to the bedroom. Once we step inside, she turns on the bedside lamp and looks at me over her shoulder. "Can you unzip me?"

My steps feel sluggish as I walk toward her. Lifting her hair, I gather it all to one side and place it over her left shoulder. "How did you get this on without me?" I reach for the zipper.

"Talent, I guess." Her tone is light and carefree, something I'm getting to see more and more of from her.

"And now?" I ask, bending to place a kiss on her bare skin as I continue to lower the zipper.

"Now you've seen me in the dress, and there's no point in twisting myself into a pretzel to surprise you."

I keep my eyes on her exposed skin as the zipper continues to lower. I can't resist running my index finger up her spine once finished. "Do you need more help?"

"You know, I might."

"Tell me what you need, Brogan?" My voice is husky and full of desire for her.

"My bra, can you unhook that for me?" she asks. Her voice is soft and hesitant, but she still speaks up to tell me what she wants.

My hands move to her bra, and I unhook it easily. "What about this?" I say, tugging her dress at her shoulders. "Do you need help with this?"

She glances at me over her shoulder, and her big green eyes are full of need. "Do you mind?"

"Anything for my wife." Slowly, I peel her dress off each shoulder, and it pools at her waist. Her bra is strapless, and it falls to the floor when she lifts her arms. "How's that?" I ask, my hands skimming her sides.

"I might need more help," she says. Her voice shakes with her nerves.

I kiss her bare shoulder. "We can stop if this is too much."

"No." She shakes her head as if her no doesn't get her point across. She turns to face me, and it takes every ounce of willpower inside me to keep my eyes on her face and not her bare tits.

I don't know what I'm expecting, but it's not for her to shimmy her hips and let her dress fall to the floor. This time, I can't hold back. My eyes scan her from head to toe. She's in nothing but a pair of black silk panties, and my mouth waters, while my cock presses painfully against the zipper of these black jeans I'm wearing.

"Tell me," I husk.

"I think I still need some help."

"My help?" I need her to spell it out for me. The last thing I want to do is scare her off after all the progress we've made.

"Only yours, Maddox."

"Only mine." I drop to my knees, place my hands on her hips, and press a kiss to her quivering belly. I peer up at her to find her watching me. "You're beautiful, Brogan." Her lips quirk up in a shy smile, and that's my cue to keep going. I grip her silk panties and pull. They slide over her hips and thighs with ease. As she steps out of them, I toss them to the side.

"Brogan," I rasp. I can smell her arousal.

"Show me."

"Show you what, baby?"

"Show me what you want to do to me."

"So many things," I tell her. My lips find their way to her soft skin, just above her pussy. She sucks in a breath, causing me to pull back and peer up at her. "We don't have to."

"I want to. I just... I don't know how far...." Her voice trails off.

"You hold all the power here, Brogan. You tell me what you want, and that's what you'll get. Nothing more, nothing less. This is all you."

"No one has ever touched me... there. Just you."

I swallow hard. I know how big this is for her. She's putting her trust in me, something she doesn't give easily. "How about we get into bed?" I suggest. I need to slow this down. I know she wants this, but does that mean she's ready? I need to give her some time to change her mind.

"Oh." Her hands cover her breasts, and she looks like I slapped her.

"Hey." I scramble to climb to my feet. "Not because I don't want to. I want you to be comfortable. I thought the bed might be better. You might not feel so exposed under the covers."

"Right. Of course."

"Brogan, I could devour you for hours, baby, and I am not tired of tasting, looking at, or feeling you, but we have time to take this slower. I don't expect anything."

"Are you going to get into bed like that?" She nods to where I'm still fully clothed.

"You want to help me?" I ask.

She nods, and I drop my hands to my sides. I watch as she raises her shaky hands and fumbles to unbutton my shirt. Needing to be connected to her, I grip her hips and pull her closer. She laughs, and that seems to help ease some of her nerves as she manages to finish the last button and push my shirt from my shoulders. It falls to the floor, and I reach behind my neck, grabbing my T-shirt and chucking it.

"You still have work to do." I wink at her, and she smiles, her shoulders relaxing even further.

She moves to the button of my jeans and makes quick work of the button and zipper. She grips my waistband and tugs, taking my boxer briefs and jeans at the same time.

"Oh," she says, surprised, when my hard cock slaps against my bare abs.

"All for you," I tell her.

I kick at my jeans until they're off and flying across the bedroom. Brogan stands before me. Her gaze is zeroed in on my cock.

"Does it hurt?"

"Not in a bad way."

"Can I?"

I slide my hand behind her neck, and she looks at me. "Anything you want, Brogan."

She reaches out and grips me.

"Tighter," I instruct. She tightens her hold, and I groan at the feel of her soft hands around me.

"Are you sure I'm not hurting you?" she asks.

I bite the inside of my cheek, and shake my head. I need to give her this time to explore, but fuck me, I'm ready to lose control. Needing a distraction, I lift my hand to her breast, running the pad of my thumb over her hard nipple. She closes her eyes and tilts her head back, never letting go of my cock that she's softly stroking.

"Bed, baby."

She releases me and dives for the bed, climbing under the covers, and I follow her, pulling her naked body against my own. "You were made for me," I tell her, running my hands over her.

"Why do you say that?"

"Because I've never craved the feel of someone's skin pressed to mine. I've never almost come from a woman touching my cock."

"You mean—" She stops talking as if she's embarrassed to say the words.

"That's exactly what I mean."

"You can, you know. Do that."

"Not until you do." No way in hell do I come first.

"I don't know if I can. I mean, I don't know how." Her cheeks turn that adorable shade of pink that I love so much.

"You can. I promise you that you can. My hands, my mouth, and my cock... they can all make you come."

"I don't know."

I'm unsure if she's saying she doesn't know if I'm right or believes me. Either way, I have to reel myself in and think about unsexy things to keep myself in check. "Do you want me to show you?" She's quiet for a long time, and I'm ready to tell her it doesn't have to be tonight when she answers me.

"Only if you show me you too."

"You want me to come?"

"Yes."

"After you."

"Maddox—" she starts, and I know she's second-guessing this.

I reach over and turn off the bedside lamp before pulling her back into my arms. "Tonight, we sleep like this." I pull her closer, my hard cock pressing against her belly. "Baby steps."

"I'm sorry." She presses her forehead to my chest.

"You have nothing to be sorry for. You've given me a piece of you that no one else has, and I'll cherish it."

"But you're... ready."

"I'll be fine. Right now, I want to hold my wife and enjoy her skin pressed to mine while we drift off to sleep."

"This feels... nice," she whispers.

"Yeah," I agree. We're quiet and her breathing starts to even out. "Happy Valentine's Day, baby."

"Happy Valentine's Day." Her body relaxes into mine and her breathing is deep and even.

"Maddox?"

"Yeah?"

"I'm glad it was you. If I had to wake up married to someone, I'm glad it was you."

I smile into the darkness of the room. "Only me, Brogan."

"Only you," she says softly, before drifting off to sleep.

I stay awake, holding her, running my fingers through her hair, talking my cock down, but I wouldn't change it. We're making strides toward our future. She's taking pieces of me she doesn't know are hers, but that's okay. One day soon, I'll be able to tell her how she has all of me, in all the ways that matter.

BROGAN 11

"How are things?" Susan, my therapist, asks me. We're sitting in matching chairs in her office.

"They're going." I smile, because I can't help myself.

"That's new." Susan points to my face.

"Yeah," I agree. I'm way past trying to hide things from this woman. Besides, hiding doesn't help me get over the past and look toward the future.

"How's married life?"

"It's... not at all what I anticipated, and more than I ever dreamed." I'm aware that I'm gushing over my husband, but I can't seem to help myself.

"You're what? Ten weeks into your agreed time frame?"

"Yeah, something like that."

"How do you feel about that?"

"The timeline?"

"Yes."

"I feel like six months isn't enough time."

"Enough time for what, Brogan?"

I fight the urge to roll my eyes. I know what she's doing, and it's annoying as much as it's helpful. "Not enough time with him," I whisper.

"You want more time with him?"

"Yeah." I sigh.

"Have you told him that?"

"No. I don't plan to tell him either." I can't tell him that I cherish every minute I spend with him.

"Tell me why."

"What if he changes his mind?" That's what scares me the most. I didn't know my mother, but I felt the loss of her my entire life. Losing my dad gutted me, but I didn't really have time to grieve, because I was helping my sister raise two tiny baby girls on her own. That's something that Susan has helped me understand, Briar too. We didn't get to grieve our father. However, Forrest, he helped Briar leap over her worries of losing him, but I'm still stuck in my head.

I care about Maddox. He holds a piece of me. No man before him ever has, and to have him walk away, or worse, lose him, I wouldn't survive that. I feel that deep in my soul. It's been a little over two months being married to him, and he's the best part of my day.

Every day.

"Brogan, do you really think he's going to change his mind? From everything you've told me, Maddox adores you."

"I don't know. That's what my head tells me."

"What does your heart tell you?"

The silence rings between us. Closing my eyes, I really think about her words. I think about our time together. I think about how patient he's been with me, and how he looks at me, like I'm his, like I light up his life. I think about how I want to fall into that look, into that feeling that I'm the only person in his world who matters. I'm just so afraid he's going to get fed up with my insecurities and my fear of losing someone else I love. Because even if I don't say the words out loud, I can admit to myself that I'm falling hard for him.

"My heart tells me he's a good man. My heart tells me he feels this as much as I do."

"Can I make a suggestion?"

"Sure, that's why I'm paying you the big bucks," I joke.

She chuckles lightly. "I'd like for you to consider having Maddox come to an appointment with you. I'd happily work a session with the two of you into my schedule. I know when you and Briar came together, it helped both of you so much. I think you should consider the same with Maddox. Open and honest communication is important for every marriage."

"It's temporary."

"Is it? From where I'm sitting, you both want this to last the test of time. Is that what you want, Brogan?"

"Of course that's what I want!" I say far too loudly, but Susan doesn't even flinch. "He's the first man I've wanted more from since that night. Now that he's mine, and I've experienced what it's like to go to sleep with his arms wrapped around me and his gruff good morning at the first light of day, why would I want to give that up?"

"I'm proud of you for admitting that."

I cross my arms over my chest, feeling more exposed than I have in a very long time. "Sorry I raised my voice," I mumble. I was out of line.

Susan waves her hand in the air. "It's nothing, and I'm used to it." She sets her notebook on the table in front of us and leans forward, resting her elbows on her knees. "Brogan, you're not broken. I know that's what you think, but that's your fear talking. Life has passed out some heavy hits, but you're stronger because of it. Does it suck? Sure. But look at Briar. She's embraced that life is what you make of it. You have to fight every day to live the life you want. You have to look past those hits and look toward what's next."

"More hits," I grumble.

"Maybe. Probably. Life is imperfect, just as we humans are. You're missing the biggest pieces of this puzzle, Brogan."

"What's that?"

"Do you want to take those hits standing alone or with a man next to you, who wants to hold you up and take each one for you? *With* you. Do you want to live in fear or let love and happiness guide you?"

I let her words spin around in my mind. I know she's right. I've spent so much time trying to make up for that night at the frat party. The guilt sits heavily on my shoulders, and I don't deserve a man like Maddox. I don't deserve that love and happiness.

"Our time's up for today, but think about what you want. Really think about it. It's going to be a fight every day. Also, consider inviting Maddox to an appointment. You let me know when and we'll make it work."

"Thank you, Susan." I stand and move toward the door.

"Brogan?"

I turn to look at her.

"It's not your fault." She smiles, and I give her a half-assed one in return. She tells me this at the end of every solo appointment. I might not always talk about that night, but that's where my guilt lies. Susan, I'm sure, plans to keep telling me until I believe her.

I don't know if I ever will.

⸻

When I make it to the house, Maddox is already home. As I step inside, I can smell he's already working on dinner. After kicking off my shoes and hanging up my coat, I go in search of my husband.

"Hey, beautiful. How was your day?" He offers me a huge smile, one I've noticed he only gives me.

"Good. I worked until noon, since I work Saturday, and had a therapy appointment after."

"How did that go? Anything you want to talk about?" he asks.

I don't know why, but his question has tears springing to my eyes. I feel raw after every session, but this feels different. I shake my head, unable to form words. Maddox puts the lid back on the pot, turns off the burner of what smells like chili, and, in a few long strides, he's standing before me. He doesn't say a single word; he just wraps his arms around me and holds me close. His arms band around me like a vise, and no matter how hard I try, I can't keep my tears from falling.

My arms go around him, and I fist his shirt as the tears continue to flow. Maddox never loosens his hold on me. He kisses my head, and his grip holds strong as he lets me work through my tears. When I try to pull away, he grunts, and the next thing I know, his hands are on the backs of my thighs, and I'm wrapping my legs around his waist, before burying my face in his neck.

I'm embarrassed. I'm an emotional wreck, and this man doesn't deserve to deal with my drama. We're moving, but I can't find it inside me to care where we're going. When I feel him sit, I finally open my eyes. We're on the couch.

I lift my head and wipe at my eyes. I part my lips to apologize, but Maddox places his index finger over them. "Come here." He pats his chest, and I lie against him. It's a little awkward, but we make it work.

He runs his hands up and down my back and pushes my hair out of my face. "You don't have to tell me, but, baby, my heart is cracked wide open right now. I hate seeing your tears. I want to fix whatever's bothering you so I can see those big green eyes light up with your smile."

"I told you I'm broken, and I soaked your shirt." I don't know why, but that bothers me. He's such a good man. He's going to get tired of my bullshit soon; I'm certain.

"No." His voice is stern. "You're not broken. You're hurting, Brogan. Those are two very different things."

"What makes you think I'm hurting?" I ask, fighting off another round of tears.

"Because you're my wife. It's my job to know. I live with you. I sleep next to you. I'm spending my life with you. I'd know if you're broken, and, baby, that's not it. You have a lot going on up here." He taps my temple. "And in here." He rests that same hand over my heart. "I'm here when you're ready. Until you are, come to me and let me hold you. You can soak as many shirts as you need to as long as you're in my arms when you do it."

I'm quiet for a long time, and Maddox lets me sit with my thoughts. "I miss my dad."

"I can't imagine that pain," he replies softly.

"He was all we had."

"That's not true anymore. You have an entire group of people, an Everlasting Ink family, who love you. You, Briar, and the girls. You have me."

"I feel that here." I tap his chest over his heart. "But it's this"—I lift my hand and tap his temple—"that needs to catch up."

"Did you talk about your dad today?" he asks gently.

"Not really. We talked about you."

"Me?" he asks, surprised.

"Yeah."

"Okay."

I study him. "That's it? Okay?"

"I don't know what else to say, Brogan. I want you to talk to me. I want you to trust that I'm here for you, but I can't make you do that. Whatever you talk to your therapist about is yours and yours alone. I hope you know that you can talk to me, but I'm not going to pressure you to tell me. Just... am I causing your pain?" His hand again goes to my chest, to rest over my heart. "Am I causing these tears?"

"No," I rush to say. "It's me, and my hangups with my past and our present."

He nods, but the sadness and worry I see in his eyes has me parting my lips to tell him more. "Susan, that's my therapist, Briar's too. Anyway, she suggested I bring you to a visit with me."

"When do we go?"

"Just like that?" I ask, tilting my head to the side to study him.

"Yes. Just like that. If that's what you need. If you want me there, then I'm there. Tell me when, and I'll make it work."

I smile at that. "That's what Susan said. She told me she would work us into her schedule."

"When?" he asks again.

"I—I'm not sure." It's not that I don't want him to go with me, but does that end us? Does that let him see what the next fifty years he keeps talking about will look like? Living with a wife who's dealing with crushing guilt that keeps her from truly living. That's what Susan says, but she thinks I can overcome it. I'm just not so sure that I can.

He places his hands on my cheeks. "When you know, you let me know. There is nothing that will keep me from being there for you."

Tears well again. "Thank you, Maddox."

He sits up, bringing us closer together, his hands still cradling my cheeks. "I'm all in, Brogan. These past few weeks have been better than I ever could have imagined them to be. I want this life with you. Together, we'll fight through whatever battles we have to face to make that happen."

Until he gets tired of the battle, my head says, but my heart... it melts for this man, for my husband.

"I don't deserve you."

"You deserve everything," he says, kissing me softly. "Are you hungry?"

I nod. "Something smells amazing."

"I made chili. I was only on the books for half a day today. I work late tomorrow night, so I wanted to be here when you got home to spend the night with you."

"You're spoiling me."

"I care about you." He shrugs. "Spoiling comes with that." He winks.

"You make the bad days better," I confess.

His eyes light up as if I just told him he won a million dollars. I try to move off his lap, but he locks his arms around me, holding me in place.

"You, wife, are the best part of every day." He kisses me again, this time deeper, and I open for him, saying with my kiss what I don't have the guts to tell him with my words.

I'm falling for you.

I want you.

He slides his hands under my sweater, and I rock against him. I grip his shirt, holding him close. I'm new to all of this, but kissing my husband is something I've come to crave. No matter how many kisses we share, I want more. No matter what happens, there will never be a time when I don't want more of Maddox Lanigan.

He groans and tears his lips from mine. "Dinner," he says, resting his forehead against mine. "I made dinner."

"Dinner. Right," I say, catching my breath.

Maddox laughs. "Let me feed you."

I nod, and this time, when I try to climb off his lap, he lets me. I offer him my hand, and he takes it, letting me help him stand from the couch even though he doesn't need the help. He laces our fingers together and leads me to the kitchen.

We enjoy dinner sitting at the kitchen island, talking about our day. Maddox finished a chest piece for a long-time customer this morning, and I told him about the patient that fainted on me when I tried to draw his blood.

"You know, it's always the men," I tell him. "Big babies."

He laughs. "Trust me, I know. I get these big-ass burly guys coming in for ink, and as soon as they see my needle, their eyes are rolling back in their heads."

"Do they go through with it?"

"Usually. I have a regular who brings an eye mask. He lays down and puts it on with headphones, and that's how he stays until I'm done."

"That's dedication." I laugh.

"It is," he agrees.

"Briar and I always said we were going to get matching tattoos, but we've never taken the plunge."

His eyes burn with intensity when he says, "If that happens, you have to let me do it."

"I'm sure any of the guys will be fine. You're all super talented."

"No." He shakes his head. "No way. If my wife is getting ink for the first time, it's going to be from me."

"You're bossy," I tease.

"Promise me, Brogan."

"Is this really that important to you?" I ask.

"Yes."

"Fine. If we ever decide to go through with it, I'll let you do it."

"Trust me, Forrest will be the same way."

"So, they won't match, if they're done by two different people," I tell him. I know that's not true. They'd use the same template, and like I said, they're all hella talented from the pictures I've seen, but I know it will rile him up. I've never had a man be jealous over me, and I'm pretty sure that's where this conversation veered off to.

"Brogan," he growls, and I giggle.

"I'm just teasing."

He leans in and kisses me. Sliding his hand behind my neck, he presses his forehead to mine. "It drives me crazy to think of another man marking you."

"It's just a tattoo."

"It's forever, baby. I'm the only man who gets to be a part of your forever."

"And what if you weren't a tattoo artist?" I counter. I'm enjoying this way too much after the heavy of the day.

"I'm sure I'd feel differently, but I'd still need to be there, and it would have to be in a location on your body where you don't have to strip down."

"Oh, so not on my breasts."

"Brogan." Another warning growl follows, which makes me laugh.

"I'm teasing."

"You're giving me an ulcer," he says, dead serious.

"I'm sorry." I lean in and kiss him. I don't initiate our kisses often, and I love how his eyes sparkle when I do. "Forgive me?"

"Like I could ever stay mad at you. All you have to do is bat those big green eyes at me, and I'm toast."

"So, if I do this?" I bat my eyes at him. "And ask for more kisses."

He stands and lifts me from my chair, tossing me over his shoulder. "My wife gets what my wife wants," he says, marching off toward the bedroom.

"We need to clean up."

"I'll take care of it. First, I'm running you a bath, and I'm going to kiss the hell out of you while I do. Then you're going to soak in the tub while I clean up, and later, you can have all the kisses."

"All of them?" I tease.

"Forever," he promises, and there's something in his gaze, something in the intensity of his words that makes me almost believe him.

MADDOX 12

"YOU WANT ONE?" LEGEND OFFERS me a beer.

"Nah, I told the wife she could drink." I hold up my bottle of water.

Legend grins. "How is the wife?"

"Fucking perfect." I glance around, making sure no little ears are close by to hear my declaration. I need to work a little harder at cleaning up my potty mouth, especially when the kids are around.

"Yeah," Legend agrees. "Just wait until you add a kid to the mix. It's unlike anything else, man."

I follow his eyes, and he's watching his wife, Monroe, and their son, Kane, who was born four months ago. "That's what I hear." I nod toward Roman and Forrest, sitting on the living room floor with Lilly and the twins, River and Rayne, playing with blocks.

"It won't be long and they'll be having another one," Legend says.

"Which one?" I ask, because today is Lilly's second birthday, and I know Roman wants more, and Forrest, he'd have a houseful if Briar was on board, and who knows, she might be. If there was ever a man meant to be a father, it's Forrest. Hell, all of them. I'd even go as far as to say that about Lachlan and me as well, but we're not there yet. Well, he's not. I'd knock my wife up tonight if she would let me, but she needs time, and that's okay. We'll get there. I believe that with all that I am. If I'm ever a father, it will be because Brogan Lanigan made me one.

"Both of them." Legend laughs.

"What about you?" I ask him.

"Yeah, as soon as Monroe's ready."

I watch as Monroe hands Kane to Brogan and says something before moving down the hall. "I'll be right back."

"Bring my son back with you," Legend calls after me.

I wave over my shoulder as I make my way toward Brogan and baby Kane. "Hey," I say, offering Kane my finger, and he latches on, giving me a gummy smile. "Look at you, little man. Growing like a weed," I tell him.

"He's the sweetest," Brogan says, smiling down at the baby in her arms.

"You need one of those," Lachlan says, joining us.

"We need a couple, but we're in no hurry," I tell him.

"Maybe you'll have twins. That'd be cool. Three sets of twins in the family." Lachlan nods like it's the best news he's heard all day.

"Maybe Forrest and Briar will have twins," I tell him.

Lachlan grins and points his index finger at me. "Four sets. Hell yeah, that's cool as hell."

"What's cool as *h e* double hockey sticks?" Forrest asks. He has a daughter on each hip.

"Twins," Lachlan replies, keeping his answer basic, not to confuse River and Rayne, making them think there is going to be another set of twins.

"I'm a twin," River says.

"Me too," Rayne says, laying her head on Forrest's shoulder.

"That's right. Just like Mommy and Aunt Brogan," Forrest tells them.

"Come here, Rayne. Uncle Maddox needs some of that love." I reach for her and she comes into my arms, resting her head against my shoulder, just like she did with her dad.

"Me too. Hand her over, Daddy. You're a daughter hog." Lachlan holds his arms out.

"Daddy's a daughter hog," River repeats with a giggle as she holds her arms out for Lachlan to take her.

"Daddies do that," Roman says, joining us, bouncing Lilly on his hip.

"We need more babies," Forrest grumbles.

"I'm taking mine," Legend says, reaching for Kane.

Brogan turns, blocking him. "I just got him," she whines.

"I lost mine too," Forrest tells him.

"Who's going to even this up? We need two more. Mad? Lach? Rome? Forrest?" Legend asks.

"What are we talking about?" Monroe asks. She looks at Brogan. "Want me to take him?"

"No." She smiles at her friend, and my heart squeezes. I love seeing her like this. It's easy to imagine it's our baby in her arms. Fuck me, I can't wait for that day.

"We need more babies," Legend tells Monroe, stepping behind her and wrapping his arms around her waist.

She leans into him. "Not it." She laughs. "I just need a few more months, then we can talk." Legend whispers something in her ear, making her blush.

"I think Lilly needs a little brother," Monroe says as Emerson joins our little huddle, snuggling up to her husband.

"Why are we all huddling on this side of the room? And a little brother or little sister, I'd take either," Emerson adds with a shrug.

"Baby girl?" Roman speaks up. "We have a room full of babysitters." The way he's looking at her, I fear she might get pregnant by immaculate conception.

"Gah! Stop that!" Forrest covers his ears, making us laugh. He's teasing. He's long past worried about his best friend being married to his little sister.

"And we should be next. The girls are going to be five," Forrest answers.

"What are we next for?" Briar asks. She hands each of their daughters a juice box before going to Forrest's side and snuggling against him.

"I want a baby brother," Rayne says.

"We need more boys, huh?" I ask her.

"I'd like a sister too," she tells me, and everyone laughs.

"Daddy, can we have one of each?" River asks Forrest.

"We'll see what we can do, Razzle," he says, using his nickname for her. He kisses Briar's temple, and she smiles up at him.

Briar returns his with one of her own. "We'll see," she eventually answers.

My eyes go back to my wife, only to find her watching me. She smiles and takes her eyes back to the baby in her arms.

"You ready for presents, Lilly?" Emerson asks her daughter.

"Pwesents." Lilly nods.

"Let's do it." Roman kisses her cheek and moves farther into the living room. We all follow him to find a seat. Monroe takes Kane back and sits on Legend's lap as she holds Kane on hers.

River and Rayne are on the floor with Forrest as they help Lilly with her presents. Emerson sits nearby with her camera, snapping pictures. Lachlan's in the recliner, and Briar is on the couch with Brogan and me. Lilly laughs her way through her gifts, and River and Rayne are thrilled to be able to help her open them. Lilly is still at the age that she'd rather play with the wrapping paper, but eventually, with the help of her older cousins, she makes her way through all of her gifts.

"She's such a cutie," Brogan comments.

"She really is," Briar agrees with her.

"So, is there something you need to tell me?" Brogan asks her sister.

Briar laughs. "Not yet, but maybe soon."

"Really?" Brogan asks excitedly.

"Yeah, we both want more, and the girls are going to be turning five soon. We don't want much more time between them."

"Briar." Brogan's voice cracks. "I'm so happy for you." She pulls her sister into a side hug.

"Thank you. I never knew it could be like this. There are some days I still feel like it's all going to disappear, but then Forrest wraps his arms around me, and I remember that I wouldn't trade a single moment with him. No matter what our future holds, my time with him will be here." She taps her chest.

"I'm proud of you," Brogan whispers.

Briar replies, but her voice is too low for me to hear.

"Who wants cake?" Roman asks.

"Cake!" River and Rayne climb to their feet and rush toward the kitchen.

"Girls! Don't run in the house!" Briar and Forrest call out to them at the same time, making each other laugh. Forrest offers Briar his hand and leads her into the kitchen.

I wrap my arm around Brogan and pull her onto my lap once it's just us in the living room.

"Do you not want cake?" she asks, furrowing her brow.

"I just needed to hold you for a second." I hug her tightly. I can't seem to ever get enough of her. If she's close, I need to be next to her. Something tells me that's never going to change.

"You okay?" She turns to look at me, resting her palm against my cheek.

"I'm perfect. Being here with them, and their kids, it makes me excited for us to get there. I know we're not ready yet, but it's something to look forward to, you know?"

"That's... not what I expected you to say."

"I know you need time, but as soon as you're ready, you let me know."

"Knock knock," Maggie says as she opens the front door and steps inside, ending our conversation before she can reply. "Hey, you two." She smiles when she sees us snuggled up on the couch.

"Hey," Brogan greets her. "I'm glad you could make it."

"Me too. I picked up a shift before I knew the party was today, but it was only a half a day, so I hope I didn't miss too much."

"Presents," Brogan tells her. "They're in the kitchen serving cake now."

"I could go for a nice big piece of cake after that shift. It might have only been half a day, but it was busy." Maggie chuckles and heads toward the kitchen.

"We better go before they eat it all," I tell my wife.

"Did you see the size of that cake?" Her eyes grow wide. "No way they can eat all that."

"Lachlan has a sweet tooth," I tease. It's not a complete lie, but even he can't devour that big-ass birthday cake.

Brogan laughs as she leans in and pecks a quick kiss to my lips. "Come on, you." She stands, pulls me from the couch, and I follow her into the kitchen. We make it just in time to sing "Happy Birthday" and watch Lilly devour her own little mini cake, making a mess of herself and, well, everything around her. Roman and Emerson smile as they watch her, and Emerson snaps picture after picture.

It's a great day with family and celebrating Lilly. She's not the oldest anymore, but she was our first Everlasting Ink baby. I love them all the same, but Lilly will always be the first. It's also been a day of affirmation for me. I know that Brogan is my future, and I'm certain we'll get our happy ending.

<hr>

"Just think, we get to do that again in three weeks." Brogan laughs as she sits on the couch next to me. "I can't believe River and Rayne are turning five. It feels like it was just yesterday we were bringing them home from the hospital."

"Sounds like it won't be long until they're bringing another home from the hospital."

"Yeah." She smiles. "I'm so happy for them." She leans over and rests her head on my shoulder.

"A lot has changed in a year." I think back to River and Rayne's fourth birthday party that the guys and I pretty much crashed. I mean we were invited, but I don't think they expected all five of us to show up.

"Right? It's been a good year, though."

"The best," I say, wrapping my arms around her.

"I should get up and do something before I fall asleep. There must have been something in that cake," she says, covering a yawn.

"We're napping. Nothing needs to be done right now. Here or the bedroom?"

"Here."

I manage to lie down without either of us standing up, and she takes the spot in front of me. I reach for the blanket that she keeps on the back of the couch and cover us with it.

"I think I like afternoon naps," I say, wrapping my body around her like a koala. "We should do this more often." I can definitely get on board with napping with my wife.

"I've never been much of a napper."

"That was when you were single. You're a married woman now. Saturday afternoons are reserved for cuddling your sexy husband on the couch."

"Sexy?"

"Come on, baby, you know you think I'm sexy."

"Compared to who? Have you seen Lachlan's abs?" she teases.

I swat her ass and she giggles. "Saturday afternoons are reserved for naps with my sexy husband."

"Damn right, they are." I press my lips to her forehead and close my eyes.

⁂

The house is dark when I open my eyes. "Hey," Brogan rasps, her voice still laced with sleep.

"We must have been tired. I blame you. You're all warm and snuggly."

She laughs. "I could say the same thing about you."

"Are you hungry? I can make us something," I ask her. My stomach growls, making us laugh.

"Why don't we just order pizza?" she suggests, sitting up.

"Yeah, that sounds good." I reach for my phone on the coffee table and pull up the contact for the local pizza place. "Call it in."

"Our usual?" she asks.

I love that we have a usual and the comfort level we've reached with one another. "Yep." She makes the call and tosses my phone back to the table and stands. "I need to get out of these jeans." She curls up her nose. "Remind me on our next nap to not sleep in jeans."

"What I just heard was to strip you naked before we take our next nap. Noted."

"Stop." She laughs. "I'll be right back."

I stare after her as she moves down the hall toward our bedroom. I move to sit up, and my jeans are tight around my cock, because, of course I'm hard. I just had my wife nestled up against me for over two hours. I wince as I stand, and the zipper of my jeans presses painfully against my hard length. "My wife is smart as hell. No more naps with jeans," I mutter as I make my way to our room to change into some sweats.

When I step into our bedroom, Brogan is sliding a pair of pajama pants over her hips. "Damn, I'm late."

She points a finger at me. "No funny business. The pizza will be here soon, and from the sounds coming from your belly, you need nourishment."

She's not shying away from me. "If you think you're not nourishment, baby, I'm doing something wrong." I wink at her.

"Stop." She snickers and covers her face with her hands.

"You want me to show you?" I ask her.

"Maddox!"

I shrug. "You brought it up."

"I did not." She shakes her head, a smile playing on her lips. "I'm going to go wait for the pizza."

I give her time to get one step out of the door before I call after her. "Fine! You can be dessert."

"Oh my God!" She laughs and sprints down the hall.

I quickly change out of my jeans and join her in the living room. She has music playing on the Bluetooth speaker and is scrolling through her phone.

I walk up to her and hold my hand out for her. "Ma'am."

She peers up at me, setting her phone to the side. "Yes?"

"Dance with me."

"Here?" She glances around the living room.

"Were you more interested in a mattress tango instead?" I wag my eyebrows.

"What am I going to do with you?" She chuckles, placing her hand in mine, allowing me to pull her off the couch and into my arms. "Dance With You" by Brett Young begins to play, and it couldn't be more perfect.

"Dance with me." I smile down at her, tugging her close. I don't want an inch of space between us as I sway to the beat and softly sing the lyrics in her ear. She melts into me, which has me closing my eyes and memorizing this moment. Maybe we should make this an after-nap tradition too. I'm down for anything that keeps her in my arms.

She might not be able to say it yet, but I feel it. I feel her opening up to me more and more every day, and I can see our future so clearly. There are so many more nights like this. Just the two of us hanging out together, barefoot and dancing in our pajamas. Then, days like today where we spend time with our family, and so much more. Our kids are dancing around us. I see it all like a vivid movie reel in my mind.

When the song ends, she lifts her head, and there are tears swimming in her eyes, but her smile lights a fire inside my soul. I move my hands to cradle her cheeks and kiss her. I take my time tasting her, showing her that this is one of the moments. One that we'll cherish and look back on for years to come.

When the doorbell rings, I groan and my wife chuckles. "You need food."

"I was holding my food," I counter.

"Your food is hungry." She kisses the corner of my mouth and pulls away to get the door.

I tug her back into me and crush my mouth to hers. The doorbell rings again, and I force myself to release her. "What about now?"

"What?" she asks, dazed.

"Are you still hungry?"

She nods. "Pizza. Right. I have to get the pizza." She pulls away, and this time, I let her go. I grab us drinks, paper plates, and napkins so we can eat in the living room and start that new series she's been talking about. We talk and laugh, and eat way too much, and it's the best night. One I hope we'll repeat over and over again.

BROGAN 13

"READY?" MADDOX ASKS AS WE pull in front of the building and park. He's practically bouncing in his seat.

"I'm ready." I smile at him and his enthusiasm. He reminds me of the girls at Christmas or their birthday.

"I can't wait to show you." He reaches for his handle and looks back at me. "Stay put."

I salute him. "Sir, yes, sir." I laugh.

His eyes heat. "You can't get me all turned on before I show you around," he says, before climbing out of the truck and skipping to my side. He literally skips to get to my door, and his smile is infectious. "I can't believe this is the first time you're seeing it." He nods toward the new Everlasting Ink building we're parked in front of.

"Well, I'm here now, and I'm excited to see it."

He grins, links his fingers with mine, and leads me inside. "Where is everyone?" I ask him.

"We're early. Like an hour early." He chuckles. "I just wanted time with you to show you around. So, this is the entrance." He grins, waving his hands around the grand waiting room. "That's where Drake and Lyra will work. We're probably going to need to hire more people, considering we have more space for guest artists to work."

"How does that work?"

"The shop has gained a lot of recognition over the years. We have artists reaching out all the time wanting to do a guest spot. It's more to help get their name out there. We require them to submit their work, and we vet them before agreeing to let them come to work in our shop. We've built this place on blood, sweat, and tears, and we aren't willing to let someone who is shit at tattooing come in and tarnish our name."

"So, they come and work for an undetermined amount of time?"

"Sometimes it's a day, a weekend, a week, or even longer. It just depends on the situation. We didn't really have room for it at the current shop, but we built extra rooms to allow for it here. We get a lot of walk-ins, and our lists are out six months and longer, so having guest artists come in helps keep that under control."

"That's amazing, Maddox. I'm so proud of you. Of all of you."

He pulls me into his chest and wraps his strong arms around me. I feel his lips press to my temple. "Thanks, babe. Come on. I want to show you the rest." He leads us down the hall, pointing out offices, and the guest artists' offices. "This is the kids' playroom," he says, pushing open a door.

"You have a playroom for the kids?" I ask, surprised.

"Yeah, I mean, our family is growing, and if the guys ever need to bring the kids to work with them, we wanted a safe place for them to be. It has its own bathroom and tub. That was Roman's idea. Something about diaper blowouts." He chuckles. "Through that door there are a couple sets of bunk beds and some baby beds too. This is the play area."

"Maddox, this is incredible." I walk over to the three small vanities that I know my nieces would love to play dress-up at.

"That was Emerson's idea. She thought Lilly, River, and Rayne would enjoy dressing up."

"They'll love it. You all have embraced them as a part of your family. I can't tell you what that means to me, and I know Briar too."

"They're Forrest's daughters. Of course they're family," he says, not missing a beat. "The workbench is for Kane, and I'm sure we'll need to add more as we add babies."

"You've thought of everything."

"We tried to. We put a lot of time and thought into this. Come on. There's more." He leads me down the hall to a large meeting room and another break room. "This is the family break room. The guest artist and staff use the other one. This is a place our wives and kids can be. It's a little extra, but we wanted it to be our space, if that makes sense."

"I love it. It's amazing."

"We have Legend to thank for all of this. The business is thriving, but he used his inheritance to purchase the land, and he refuses to let us pay him back."

"He's a good man."

"The best. He and the guys, they're my brothers."

"I love that for all of you."

"Okay, let's go to my office." He flashes me a playful grin before bending and tossing me over his shoulder, causing me to shriek with laughter.

I smack his ass. "I know how to walk."

"Yeah, but this is more fun. You're turning me on with all of that spanking, baby."

"St—op," I say, sputtering my words filled with laughter.

When he steps inside a room, that must be his office, he slides me down his body and turns me so that my back is to his front. "This is ours."

"Ours?" I look back at him over my shoulder.

"Yeah, so this is something else that Roman and Legend insisted on. They wanted our offices to be a space for our families too. So over there"—he points to a couch and a small refrigerator with a TV—"is our little living room area or whatever you want to call it."

I step away, and he lets me as I walk around the room, taking it all in. There's a blanket in my favorite color, baby blue, draped over the back of the small couch. I move around, taking it all in, and freeze when I get to his desk. My eyes lock on a picture of us. We're both smiling. He's looking down at me, and me up at him, and we look happy. So incredibly happy.

"Where did you get this?" I ask him.

"Emerson. She took it at Lilly's birthday party. I had to have it. I wanted you here with me when I'm working."

"Maddox." My voice cracks. This man continues to surprise me at every turn.

He walks over and wraps his arms around me. "What about now?"

"What?" I ask, confused, my mind still on the fact that he took the time to print and frame a photo of us for his desk.

"Do you believe me now? Do you believe that I want you more than I've ever wanted anything? Do you understand that I want a life with you? This life we're building... I want it so bad, Brogan."

I don't know what to say, so I turn in his arms and hug him tightly. I let his words wash over me, and they build up a confidence in me I've never felt before. Maddox is open with his feelings and what he wants, and I'm not giving this a chance if I don't do the same.

Lifting my head, I find he's already peering down at me. "Will you—" I pause and lick my lips. I'm nervous, but I know I don't need to be. He's already agreed to come with me, but still saying the words causes anxiety to spike inside of me. "Will you come to an appointment with me?" I close my eyes, not wanting to see his reaction.

"Open those beautiful green eyes, wife," he murmurs.

I do and see him wearing a soft smile. "There is nothing you could ask of me that I'd say no to. Well, one thing, but I hope I never hear those words out of your mouth."

"Now, I'm curious." I chuckle, grateful for the break in the heavy.

"The *D* word, baby."

"Dick?" I blurt, and his body shakes with laughter. I know that's not what he meant, but I love to see his smile and the way his eyes crinkle in the corners.

He grips the backs of my thighs and lifts me. On instinct, I wrap my arms and legs around him. "Divorce," he says, leaning in close. "You want my dick, baby?" he asks as he trails kisses up my neck.

"That totally backfired." I tilt my head to give him better access.

"Everything I am is yours," he says, nipping at my ear.

"Kiss me."

"Yes, ma'am." His lips find mine, and just as with every kiss before this one, I melt into him. He squeezes my ass and moans when I rock my hips. I can feel his solid length beneath his jeans, nestled between my thighs. My leggings are doing nothing to hide how hard he is, and it's exhilarating to know it's because of me.

This sexy, amazing man wants me.

"Brogan," he murmurs against my lips. "Baby, we need to stop."

"Don't wanna," I say, kissing him again. He moves to the desk, placing me on it, before kissing me softly, and pulling back. He rests his hands on my cheeks and stares down at me, panting.

"This, remember how you feel right this minute, because when I get you home, we're picking this up again. If our family was not minutes away from walking in on us, baby, I'd have you stripped and laid out on my table so I can take my time tasting every inch of you."

"I'll remember," I assure him, just as someone calls out, "Marco," making us both laugh.

"That's Lachlan." Maddox chuckles. He kisses me one more time before lifting me from the desk and stepping away. He gives me a heated look as Lachlan appears in the doorway.

"Anyone else here?" he asks.

Maddox turns to answer him and Lachlan places his hands over his eyes. "Dude, put that thing away. Warn a guy, why don't you?" he says, roaring with laughter.

"You've seen my wife, right?" Maddox asks.

My face heats, but I'm also laughing. I love the way he and his friends are so close.

"I've seen her. Brogan, sweetheart, if you want to know what a real man—" he starts, but Maddox interrupts him.

"Out. Get the fuck out of here," he says, humor and something else in his tone.

"You know where to find me, Brogan."

"My wife!" Maddox calls out as Lachlan's laughter trails behind him down the hall.

I move to stand next to him, wrapping my arms around his waist.

"Mine," he says, kissing me again.

"He was messing with you."

"I know. He'd never, you'd never, but fuck, I hate even the thought of another man touching you."

My heart dances in my chest. Not a single day has gone by where he's not said something that didn't make me melt for him. I need to talk to my sister, or Emerson and Monroe. Surely, that's not normal? But when I look for signs that he's not sincere, I don't find any. Am I blinded by wanting him?

"Tell me when the appointment is, and I'll be there," he says, holding my gaze.

"Thank you."

"Anything, Brogan. I'll do anything for you."

Before I can answer, more voices ring down the hall. The others are here. "Come on, let's go celebrate you and your friends."

He weaves his fingers through mine and leads us back to the waiting room.

Everyone is here and taking in the new space. I'm introduced to Drake and Lisa, his girlfriend, and Lyra, who are both receptionists for the shop. The girls race around and once they find the playroom, they're addicted. Baby Kane takes it all in with a gummy smile as he's passed from person to person who want their chance to love on him.

There is just something about babies that makes you want to snuggle them close. The day is perfect, and all five guys are on cloud nine, pride showing in each of their expressions as they share the new space with us.

After we eat, which consisted of pizza and wings, I take all three little girls back to the playroom and sit with them. Not long after, Emerson, Monroe, Briar, and Maggie join me. Maggie has Kane in her arms and refuses to let him go.

"Nope. I had to pry him out of his daddy's arms. My turn isn't over yet," she says, making me laugh.

"So, how's married life?" Monroe asks.

"Good." I nod. "Actually, I have a question." I look at each of them and will myself to find the courage. Taking a deep breath, I go for it. "So, you all know we're giving this a try," I say, referring to Maddox and me.

"We do," all four of them answer.

"Well, he's just—too much sometimes," I confess.

"How do you mean?" Emerson asks.

"He says, well, the perfect things at the exact right time. Is there a manual?" I ask, only half joking. "I swear there has to be a manual."

"What kinds of things?" Maggie asks. "I have to live vicariously through the four of you, so I need details."

"I don't know. I asked him to go somewhere with me, and he said, 'Anything for you.' It's not just his words, but the intensity of his gaze when he says them. There are a million other instances, but that's the only one I can come up with right now."

"I've known the guys my entire life. They have been best friends since before I was born." Emerson chuckles. "I need to remind them of that," she adds with a twinkle in her eyes. "Anyway, I've been around them a lot."

"Me too," Monroe adds. "You know, as her bestie and all. I spent a lot of time at Forrest's house with Em growing up."

"They're all good men," Emerson says. "I can tell you with absolute certainty if anything comes out of their mouth, and they're being serious and not joking around, it's the truth, and you can bank on it."

"Em's right. They like to joke around and tease a lot, but when they're serious, they mean what they say. You can trust him, Brogan," she says gently.

"Trust is hard for me." They know about that night all those years ago, but we don't talk about it much. I hear Susan's voice in my head telling me maybe I should.

"Where did you ask him to go with you?" Briar asks.

"A therapy appointment."

"Brogan. Really? That's incredible." Briar squeezes my hand.

"Susan suggested it, and I gave myself some time to think about it. My heart and my head are in a battle. Maddox, he's doing and saying everything right, but I still have this heaviness that weighs on me that he's going to get fed up with having to be so patient and dealing with my insecurities." I pause, and no one says anything. It's almost as if they know I need to say more but need time to collect my thoughts.

"I really like him," I whisper.

"He's head over heels for you," Maggie speaks up. "I've probably spent the least amount of time with the two of you, thanks to my work schedule, but his eyes never leave you. No matter where you are in the room, he knows where you are." She points to each of us. "They all do it," she says. "Makes this single girl's heart hopeful that there's a man out there who will seek me out like that in my future."

"He's out there, babe," Emerson assures her.

"We found ours when we least expected it," Monroe says.

"Tell me about it." Briar laughs. "I never could have dreamed up my current life."

"That!" I point at my sister. "It's like I'm living in a fairy tale."

"You are," Monroe says gently.

"A real one," Emerson adds.

"Found them!" Roman calls out, stepping into the room. Not ten seconds later, Forrest, Legend, Maddox, and Lachlan follow along behind him.

I watch as each man goes to their wives, including mine. Lachlan settles next to Maggie and opens his arms for Kane. She sticks her tongue out at him, but hands him the baby.

"You good?" Maddox whispers just for me.

"I'm good," I whisper back.

"This is the kids' room," River says, placing her hands on her hips.

"Yeah," Rayne says, striking the same pose as her sister.

"Yeah." Lilly mocks and mimics the older two.

"We're all just big kids," Lachlan tells them.

"If you stay, you have to play with us," Rayne tells him.

"I'm babysitting, but you have an entire room to choose from."

"Uncle Roman, it's time for your hair appointment," River tells him.

"Yeah, Uncle Legend. Your hair appointment too," Rayne says, clapping her hands in excitement.

"What about me?" Forrest sticks his bottom lip out.

"Daddy, you had an appointment last night," River reminds him.

I smile, because I have no doubt he's had a lot of hair appointments.

"Fine, I'll just play with Lilly. You love Uncle Forrest, don't you, sweetheart?" Forrest scoops Lilly into his arms and pretends to fly her around the room, making her laugh.

"What about me?" Maddox asks the girls.

"Uncle Maddox, you have to wait your turn," Rayne tells him.

"Yes, ma'am," Maddox says.

That's how we spend the afternoon. In the kids' playroom at the new Everlasting Ink facility with full bellies and the company of our family. For a girl who's only had her sister and nieces for the past few years, it's nice, and sometimes overwhelming, to be a part of this group, but I won't lie and say my heart's not overflowing with love for my new Everlasting Ink family.

And my husband.

"We did it!" Legend hollers, slinging his arm over Monroe's shoulders.

"Thanks to you," Roman replies.

Legend waves him off. "I didn't work for the money. Hell, I didn't even know my inheritance existed until last year. I couldn't think of anything better to use it for."

"The kids' room was a nice touch," Briar speaks up.

"I can't believe they're all asleep at the same time," Emerson comments.

"It was my epic storytelling skills," Lachlan boasts.

He could tell the kids were winding down, and somehow, he managed to wrangle all four of them into letting him read them a story and all four crashed.

"I guess we should get them home," Forrest says, looking to Briar for guidance.

"Actually," I speak up, "is this place ready to go? Like open for business?"

"We are," Roman answers.

I look at my sister and grin, and she nods, flashing me her own smile. I turn to look at Maddox. "What about now?"

Maddox studies me for a few heartbeats and grins. "You're ready?"

I love that he knew exactly what I'm talking about without me having to tell him. "I am." I glance over at Briar. "Are you?"

"Let's do it."

"I have a picture on my phone, but I can run home and get the original," I say.

"Nah, just send me the picture and I'll get it sorted out," Maddox responds.

"What's going on?" Maggie asks.

"Briar and I have talked about getting a tattoo for years, we just have never taken the leap."

"Yeah, I think we were waiting so our husbands could be the ones to do it."

"For real?" Forrest asks. His eyes light up as if he was just told he won the lottery.

"Yep." Briar bobs her head.

"What are we waiting for?" He stands, takes Briar's hand, and pulls her to his room.

Maddox stands, lifts me into his arms, and carries me. "I can walk," I tell him, laughing.

"Yeah, and I can carry you." We step into his room, and he sets me on the tattoo table. His hands rest on my cheeks when he asks, "You're really going to let me put my mark on you?"

"I am. I'm glad it's going to be you." Gripping his shirt, I pull him toward me, and kiss him. I stop before we get carried away, pull my phone out of my pocket, and quickly send him the picture. I know Briar has one too, but I send her mine as well, just in case.

Thirty minutes later, we have a stencil that is exactly like my dad's handwriting. "Where do you want it?" Maddox asks.

Grabbing my phone, I call my sister. I can hear her phone ring and she's laughing when she answers. "Where are we getting these?"

"What about inside bicep?" I suggest.

"Perfect. Right arm," she says. "Love you, big sister."

Tears well in my eyes. "I love it, and I love you too, little sister." I end the call and look up at my husband, who is waiting patiently. "Inside bicep." I lift my arm to show him. "On my right arm."

Maddox smirks. "Take your shirt off, beautiful."

I do as he says, and lie back on the table, lifting my arm over my head. He gets to work prepping the skin and applying the stencil. "There, want to take a look?"

I shake my head. "No. I trust you."

"Brogan." My name is a rasp from his lips.

He knows I mean more than just this moment, because this man somehow knows me inside out. "I'm ready," I tell him.

He starts and immediately checks to make sure I'm okay, and I smile up at him. "I'm stronger than I look."

He bends down and presses his lips to mine. "I know you are, baby. But the thought of hurting you, even for this twists me up inside."

"I can have Lachlan do it," I say, knowing it will light a fire inside him.

"Yeah, that's not happening." He gives me another kiss and gets back to work.

"Why the right arm?" he asks. "Is there some kind of significance?"

"Kind of, but not really. Briar and I always said we would put our maiden name on one side, and our married name on the other." I wait for him to reply, but it never comes. "We had a few places we talked about, but we always said the left was closer to our heart. To the man we chose to give our hearts to if that day ever came."

"Beautiful and smart," he says.

I close my eyes and let him work. Time seems to fly because before I know it, he's telling me he's done, and helping me sit up. I move to stand in front of the full-length mirror and tears prick my eyes.

"I love it, Maddox. Thank you." He steps behind me, wraps his arms around my waist, and kisses my neck.

"I'm glad you love it. Come on. Let's go check on Briar."

I quickly put my shirt back on, and we go to see how things are progressing with my sister, but I already know. She's getting two tattoos today.

One day, that will be me too.

MADDOX 14

EVERYTHING IN MY LIFE IS brighter with Brogan in it.

Today was incredible, not just because my best friends and I got to show our family our new space, but because I got to share it with her. I'm stoked about the new facility and to watch our business grow. However, I'm more excited about the way my wife is staring at me as we stand at our kitchen island. I grabbed us both a bottle of water as soon as we got home.

She smiles shyly as she sips her water. No words are shared between us, but I know what she's thinking. I made her a promise earlier, and from the glint in her eye, she wants me to follow through on that promise.

I intend to, but I also don't want to push her. Even with the desire in her eyes, I can still see the apprehension as well, and I need her to understand that whatever happens between us tonight, it's all about her. She calls all the shots.

"What's that look?" she asks. Her eyes never leave mine.

"Do you remember?" I ask. I know damn good and well by the way she shifts her stance that she most definitely remembers.

"Remember what?" She tilts her head to the side, and there's a challenging glint in her eyes.

I fucking love how she's coming out of her shell with me. That turns me on more than anything to know that I'm earning her trust. Measured steps carry me to her side of the island. I don't stop until I'm standing behind her, with my hands on her hips and my lips trailing down her neck.

"What about now? Do you remember?" My lips glide across her silky-smooth skin and goose bumps break out.

"I think I'm starting to remember," she murmurs.

"Turn around."

She does as I ask, and I lift her so that she's sitting on the island. I step closer, and she widens her legs, making room for me to be nestled between her thighs. My lips find hers as my hands roam over her body. I trace her thighs with my hands, letting them roam, and I wish like hell she was naked so I could feel her soft skin.

"Is this how it starts?" she asks breathily.

"How what starts?" I ask, sliding my hand under her sweater.

"The tasting every inch of me." Her words are soft but do nothing to hide the desire in her tone.

I swallow hard. "Is that what you want?" I know that's what I said, but beyond some touching and kissing, that's as far as we've let things go.

"A promise is a promise." She looks down at the island. "I guess this is similar to your tattoo table." She smiles.

I can't help it. I toss my head back in laughter. I love this side of her. The side that's open and not afraid to tell me what she wants, because all I want is her.

"That was the only option at the time. We have better choices here." I lift her into my arms, bridal style, and carry her to our room.

"Why are you always carrying me?" she asks.

"You're my queen," I tell her.

"I don't know what to say when you talk like that," she confesses. Her tone is light, and she sounds happy.

"There is nothing to say. It's a fact. This is me, Brogan. This is me showing you that you're the most important person in my life." It's more than I've said about my feelings for her. Feelings that are so fucking big. My chest feels full, so full it could burst, but I can't tell her that. Not yet. Soon. Soon, I'll tell her that she holds every piece of me in the palm of her soft hands.

"You kiss me," I tell her.

A smile tugs at her lips. "I do like kissing you."

"Bring me those lips," I tell her, setting her down on the bed, and kissing her with everything I have. I bury my hands in her hair, holding her close. I can never get her close enough. I hope that never changes: my need for her. This time, it's my wife who takes the kiss deeper. Her tongue slides against mine, and my cock throbs for her. She whimpers when I bite down on her bottom lip, and I pull away to catch my breath.

"Wait, wasn't there supposed to be less clothing in this promise?" she asks, her voice raspy with desire.

"You trying to get me naked, wife?" I tease. Her cheeks turn a light shade of pink. I step back and stand, pulling my shirt over my head. "You better get started," I tell her.

"Okay." She nods and climbs to her feet. She starts with her leggings and pulls them over her thighs. Next, she reaches for the hem of her sweater when her eyes find mine.

"I know I should offer to turn around, but I can't seem to make myself do it. You're fucking gorgeous and mine. I'm going to watch as you reveal that tight little body to me."

She hesitates, but eventually, she slowly raises her sweater over her head and tosses it on the floor. She's left in nothing but a light pink bra and panty set. She looks every bit the innocent she is, and something inside me roars to life that it's me. I'm the man she's baring herself to. I'm the man who gets to hold her while she sleeps at night.

I'm the only one.

Possessiveness like I've never felt roars through my veins. "Beautiful," I say, reaching for the waistband of my jeans and stripping out of them and my boxer briefs all in one go. My hard cock bounces against my abs and captures her attention.

"Can I...?" she asks, her voice trailing off.

I step closer and push her hair back out of her eyes. She's staring at my chest, so I carefully place my index finger under her chin and lift her gaze to mine. "Don't ask, sweetheart. Just take. I'm your husband. You have all rights to me anytime you want."

"But if you don't want it."

My lips twitch. "I want it. I want you any way that I can get you. Take what you want, Brogan."

"That's scary."

"Then tell me what you want, and I'll give it to you."

"I want what you said." She rests her forehead against my chest, and I'm certain she's staring down at my cock, which jerks being this close to her.

"Say the words, baby. I don't want to have any miscommunications between us."

"S-Stripped naked, and the rest."

"What's the rest?" I ask her, partly because I just want to hear her say the words and the other to make sure this is what she wants. I'd never forgive myself if I pushed her too far, too fast.

"Tasting every inch of me." Her voice is so low that I barely hear her. She reaches behind her back and unhooks her bra. There's a tremble in her hands as she slides one strap, then the other over her shoulders and lets the material fall to the floor between us.

"On the bed," I tell her. My voice is gravelly and deep with desire.

I'm expecting her to lie on the bed, but instead, she sits on the edge. I can work with this. I drop to my knees before her and lift her left leg. I kiss the top of her foot and slowly trail kisses until I reach her mid-thigh. A quick glance and I see her staring down at me, with a heated gaze I've yet to see from her. Fueled by her reaction, I release the left leg and give the same attention to the right.

This time, when I reach her mid-thigh, I lift my head and place a kiss on her quivering belly. "You still with me, gorgeous?" I ask her.

She bobs her head.

"Do you want me to stop?"

This time, it's a shake of her head to answer. I don't push her for her words. Her chest rises rapidly with each breath, and I can smell her arousal. She's in this. I'm in this with her, and I already know this is going to be one of those nights with her that I'll never in my life forget.

Dipping my head, I kiss the wet spot on her panties. She gasps and lifts her hips as if silently asking for me. I grip the sides of her panties, and she lifts a little higher, giving me room to pull them off her hips and down her thighs. Once they're off, I bring them to my face and inhale. Fuck me. I've never been this hard in my entire damn life.

"Did you just—" She stops because I'm already nodding.

"You're damn right I did. Fucking perfect, Brogan."

"Is... that a thing?" she questions.

I smile up at her. "It's our thing." Her shoulders relax at that. My hand moves to her pussy, and I lightly trace my thumb over her clit. "I know I promised every inch, and we'll get there, but this... I need to taste you here first."

"Oh, you um, you don't have to do that." She tries to shut her legs, but I'm between them, right where I belong.

"Is that a no?"

"It's a you don't have to," she counters.

"Wife, do I have your permission to taste your pussy?"

"M—Maddox," she purrs.

I trace my index finger through her wetness, coating myself in her arousal. "You can say no, Brogan."

"I—I don't want to say no."

"Tell me." This time I have to hear her say it. This is a boundary we've yet to cross.

"Do you like that?"

I smile. "Yeah, baby. I like that."

"I've never—no one has ever—seen me there."

"Your pussy is perfect. Is that what you're worried about? Trust me, you're beautiful everywhere. Every delectable inch of you."

"I'm nervous," she says, huffing out a nervous laugh.

"It's just me, Brogan. I'm just a husband on his knees, ready to worship his wife."

"Please," she says, and there's a note of pleading in her tone.

"If you say stop, we stop. Understand?" I wait for her to nod. "Good girl." Her eyes darken with desire, and I grin inwardly. My wife might have a praise kink. Good news for her and me that I'm the man to give her all the praise she needs.

Lifting her legs and placing them over my shoulders, I get up close and personal with her. I peer up at her, and she's watching me, chewing on her bottom lip. That's the last thing I see before I gently trace my tongue over her clit. She moans, and the sound ignites a flame inside me.

I eat at her as if she's my last meal, and ironically enough, I hope like hell that she is. I hope this is the last pussy I ever taste. I'm starved for her. When I slip one long digit inside her, she makes a noise I've never heard from her, lifts her hips from the bed, seeking more of what I'm giving her, and buries her hands in my hair. She tugs, and I can't get enough.

"Oh God," she moans.

We'll talk about that later. My name is the only one she should be calling out for. Me. Her husband. Her walls contract around my finger, so I slide in another, and curl them slightly. Out of nowhere, she cries out, and her arousal flows across my tongue.

When her grip loosens, I place a tender kiss over her and lift my head. Her eyes are hooded as she watches me wipe my mouth with the back of my hand.

She doesn't speak, and neither do I. Instead, I gently place her legs back down and nod for her to move up the bed. She does so slowly, her body still coming down from her orgasm.

I'm quick to climb into bed next to her and pull her into my arms. Her breathing is still labored, her body is flushed, and she has this dopey, satisfied look in her eyes. I press my lips to the top of her head as I try to regulate my own breathing.

This was a huge step for her. I know that. I know the trust she had to give me to have this kind of access to her. Hope wells in my chest. I think my wife might be falling in love with me.

Once she's recovered, she asks quietly, "What about you?"

"What about me?" I know what she means. My cock is throbbing, aching for attention, but I ignore it.

"Don't you need... relief?" she asks.

"I just need you," I tell her, kissing her forehead.

"I can—" she starts, but I'm already shaking my head.

"Not tonight. I promised you something, and I delivered. There were no other promises made."

"I can help you."

"You don't have to."

"I want to." She reaches between us and grips my cock.

I have to fight to keep my eyes from rolling into the back of my head at the feel of her soft hand gripping me.

She takes her time, leisurely stroking me, and normally, that wouldn't be enough, but I'm too keyed up. Her taste is still on my lips, and her hand is on my cock. Resting my palm on her cheek, I kiss her. I try to show her with each brush of my tongue against hers how I'm feeling in this moment. I'm trying to show her that she's my everything.

Her grip strengthens and her hand moves faster. She leans down and places a kiss on my chest over my heart, and it explodes behind my rib cage.

My wife is turning me inside out.

Sitting up, she grips me tighter. Her hand on my cock has her rapt attention. While that's an image I would love burned into my mind for a lifetime, I'm looking at her. I'm watching as she chews on her bottom lip. I'm watching her chest as her breaths become shorter and faster with each one she pulls into her lungs.

I'm so close, too amped up, too lost in her to stop it. "Close," I grit. Warning her seems like the right thing to do, but she doesn't move. Her eyes never stray from what she's doing, and when she pokes her tongue out to soothe the bottom lip she's been torturing, I lose control.

I spill over into her hand and force my eyes to stay open, and fuck me, I'm glad that I did. She smiles triumphantly, effectively stealing the breath from my lungs and my heart from my chest.

They're both hers.

I can't take my eyes off her, which is why I'm able to watch as she pulls her hand to her mouth and licks her finger. The same finger that's covered in my release.

"Fuck, Brogan." I pull her down to me and kiss her.

When I finally come up for air, she wrinkles her nose. "We're both messy."

"I guess that means I better get you cleaned up." Rolling out of bed, with a mental note to change the sheets, I grab her leg and tug her to the edge, and lift her into my arms. She wraps her arms and legs around me.

We're naked, skin to skin, and nothing has ever felt better.

"Where are you taking me now?" Humor laces her voice.

"Shower."

"Together?" she asks.

"Is that okay with you?"

She nods. "I've never done that."

"It's fitting that you do with your husband." I kiss her again. "I want all of them, Brogan. Every first you're willing to give me, I want them. I'll cherish them." I pause to kiss her again. "You know what else I want?" I ask her.

"What?"

"Your last."

She relaxes into me. "I want so badly to give them all to you," she whispers.

I don't bother to hide my grin. She's mine. I feel it in my soul. This is the start of our forever.

"I think you're going to need a bigger house," I tell Forrest a week later, standing in his living room for the girls' fifth birthday party.

"I blame all of you. You spoiled them," he says, pulling his eyes from his daughters.

"Says the man who bought them matching art desks and a truckload of art supplies." Legend laughs.

"Hey, my daughters are turning five today. That's a big deal. Besides, they love my tattoos and are fascinated with drawing and coloring lately."

"Second generation of Everlasting Ink, maybe?" Lachlan asks.

"Maybe," Forrest says, wearing a grin as he watches his daughters bounce from new toy to new toy sprawled out all over their living room. Lilly chases after them, loving every minute of the time she's getting with her big cousins.

"Your wife seems awful comfortable holding my son." Legend knocks his shoulder into mine.

"She's good with kids." And she does look comfortable. She also looks beautiful. The jade green shirt she's wearing with her jeans makes her eyes pop, but to me, she looks beautiful no matter what she's wearing, and even what she's not.

"How's that going?" Roman asks.

"Good. She's—" I pause because I don't know how to describe it to them.

"Everything?" Forrest asks.

"Yeah," I agree. Everything is exactly what she is. She's the light in my life, and she's the tether that grounds me. When I asked her for six months, I knew my feelings for her would grow, but I never could have imagined this overwhelming need to consume everything she is, because that's what she's done. She's consumed me. I'm hers and always will be.

"Welcome to the club," Legend tells me.

"Thanks." Neither Brogan nor I have brought up the fact that we are less than two months away from the end of our agreed-upon six-month trial period for this marriage. I try not to even think about it because the weight of it sits heavy on my chest like a bag of bricks.

"Do they ever run out of energy?" Lachlan asks as the girls continue to play, while the ladies sit close by, keeping an eye on them.

I guess you could say we're looking over all of them where we're standing around the kitchen island.

"When they sleep." Forrest chuckles.

"Pretty much," Legend and Roman agree.

"Those little angels kept swiping the icing off the cake. They're going to be wired for hours," Lachlan says fondly.

"It's their birthday." I defend my nieces. "They can swipe all the icing they want."

"Definitely," Lachlan agrees.

"They can go home with you," Forrest jokes.

There is no way he's sending his daughters home with me. "I'll take them. They can have a sleepover with Uncle Mad and Aunt Brogan."

"You can't take them on their birthday," Forrest says, and I laugh. I know my friend far too well.

"Fair enough." I smirk, and he rolls his eyes.

Before he can reply, the girls come rushing over, with Lilly hot on their heels. "Come, draw with us," they say at the same time.

River grabs Forrest's hand and Lachlan's. Rayne takes mine and Legend's, and Roman scoops Lilly up into his arms. That's how we spend the rest of the day—drawing with the girls, while our wives and Maggie sit around and chat about.... Well, I don't know what they're talking about, but I do know that every time I look over at my wife, I find her smiling and laughing, and a happy wife is all I want.

I want her to have it all: happiness, love, and me. I'm the one who's going to give it to her.

BROGAN 15

MY HANDS SHAKE, AND MY palms are sweaty as I keep my eyes glued to the landscape passing by outside the window of Maddox's truck. When we pull up into the lot of my therapist's office, I take in a deep breath and slowly exhale, trying to calm my nerves.

"I don't have to go with you," Maddox tells me. "Babe, if this is too much for you, we can wait until you're ready."

"No. I need to do this." I turn to face him. "Susan thinks this will help, and she's helped me so much since I've started seeing her." I reach over and take his hand, and he slides his fingers between mine. "I'm not ready to lose this." I give his hand a soft squeeze.

"Brogan—" he starts, but I shake my head, cutting him off.

"Can we not? Let's just go inside."

He nods and leans over the console to kiss my lips. He drops my hand and climbs out of the truck, rushing to my side to open the door. He didn't have to tell me to stay put this time. I want to soak up as much of his attention as I can. Because things might come up today—the truth of my anxiety—and he could decide this is it. He could choose to say to hell with the rest of the weeks that we have in our agreement and walk.

I'm counting down those weeks as if the world is ending, and if I'm being honest, that's what it feels like. I can't imagine my life without Maddox. Sure, he'll still be around, but not in our house, in our bed, and not as my husband. Just the thought has pain filling my chest.

With his hand around my waist, he leads me into the building. I feel like I'm on autopilot as we step onto the elevator, and I push the button for the third floor. I can't believe I asked him to come with me. This has to be a mistake. No good can come out of him hearing more details about my broken past.

Maddox keeps me tucked into his side as we exit the elevator. I keep my head down because I feel as though I'm seconds away from losing my grip on my sanity.

I'm not ready to lose him.

It's not until I hear my name do I look up from the tile flooring. My mouth drops open and it takes me a few heartbeats to find my voice.

"Briar?"

Her eyes soften, and she smiles. "Hey."

"What are you doing here?" I can't pull my eyes away from my twin sister.

She shrugs. "I was in the neighborhood." I give her a disbelieving look, and she chuckles. "Fine. I knew you were nervous about today, and I wanted to be here for you. I'm just going to sit out here and wait, and if you need me, I'll be here." She glances at my husband, who has yet to speak but still has his arm wrapped tightly around my waist. "I know she's yours now, and I know you've got her, but I needed to be here. I could feel it here"—she places her hand over her heart—"that you needed me."

"She is mine," Maddox tells her. "But she is also yours. We're a family, and our girl needs both of us."

Tears well in my eyes. For so long, it's been Briar and me against the world, and now, here is this man who I've completely fallen for standing tall next to me, supporting me in ways I never thought possible.

Heels clicking gain our attention, and I turn to see Susan walking out of her office. "Good morning." She smiles. "Briar, I didn't know you'd be here."

"Just hanging out here in the lobby. I have a book with me." She pats her purse.

Susan nods. "Hi, I'm Susan." She offers Maddox her hand.

"Maddox Lanigan, Brogan's husband." He introduces himself, and if I'm not mistaken, there's a hint of pride in his voice.

"Nice to meet you, Maddox. Are we ready?" Susan asks us.

I nod, because I can't seem to find the words. Maddox and I move to follow Susan into her office, but I stop and turn to look at Briar. "Come with me?"

Briar is up and out of her seat and making her way toward me. She grabs my hand and leads me into the office. Susan doesn't say a word about Briar being here with us. Briar takes one of the chairs, while Susan takes the other, and Maddox and I sit on the love seat facing them.

"Maddox, I asked Brogan to invite you to a session so I could help assist her with working through telling you about some past traumas."

"Thank you," Maddox replies.

"Brogan, are you still okay if we talk freely with both Maddox and Briar here?"

"Yes." I nod and twist my hands together in my lap.

"Briar, since you are also a patient, I have to ask you the same. Are you okay to proceed with Maddox here?"

"He's my brother. Of course I am."

My eyes snap to my sister, and she smiles at me, mouthing, "I love you," and bobs her head.

Maddox reaches over and places his hand over mine. I stop twisting them together and instead open my palm, accepting his, linking our fingers together. I can already feel the calm washing over me. How he does that, I'll never know.

"I don't know how to do this," I blurt.

"That's what I'm for," Susan says gently. "Brogan, tell me how you feel."

"Broken."

"What?" Maddox turns in his seat to look at me. He studies my face, and even though I want to look away, I can't seem to force myself to do so. "Brogan, baby, you're not broken."

"Aren't I?" I counter.

"What are you afraid of, Brogan?" Susan asks.

"Losing the people I care about." My eyes fall to my lap. I can't face him or my sister.

"Loss is a part of life," Susan reminds me kindly. "What else weighs heavily on you?"

I want to yell at her to shut the hell up, but I remind myself she's just doing her job. She's here to help me, and even though she knows the answer, she's going to make me say it. Something I've never said out loud to anyone but her.

"Guilt," I mumble.

"Do you want to talk about that?" Susan asks.

No, Susan, I don't want to talk about it. "Not really," I admit, keeping the snark to myself.

"Brogan." Briar's voice cracks, and I lift my head to look at her. Even from my spot across the room, I see the tears swimming in her eyes.

Something inside me breaks, as I feel my own tears burn behind my eyes. "I wanted to go that night." My voice is raspy. I swallow past the lump in the back of my throat and keep going. I knew this is what today would be, so I need to pull up my big girl pants and rip off the Band-Aid.

"I wanted to go. You didn't. You said we wouldn't know anyone, but those cute guys from the deli invited us, and I wanted to go." A hot tear rolls across my cheek. "I begged you, and you gave in because you're my sister, and you didn't want me to go alone."

I choke back a sob before continuing, "It's my fault. I never should have begged you to go to that party. We had barely graduated high school. We had no business at a college party with guys who were getting ready to graduate and that we didn't know."

Tension radiates off Maddox, but I can't look at him. I can't look at any of them, and they all remain quiet, giving me the time I need to work through these feelings that I've only ever spoken to Susan.

"I'm the older sister. I should have been more responsible. We never should have taken drinks from them, and I never should have left your side for a second." I focus on breathing because I feel like I'm on the verge of a panic attack. When I've finally calmed my breathing, I look up to find my sister with tearstained cheeks.

"What happened that night was not your fault, Brogan. We couldn't control that they drugged us. There was no way you could have stayed glued to my side, because they made sure of it. Should we not have been there? I don't know. I'd like to think that they were only four years older than us. It's not like we were hanging out with men twenty years older than us. What they did was wrong. They are the ones to blame. I hate that we'll never know who they are. I used to hate that my daughters would never have a father, but that all changed for me in the last year. I met an amazing man who gave me the time I needed to get to know him. He gave me patience and love, and he showed me that my past does not define me, or my daughters. My babies have a daddy. His blood might not be flowing through their veins, but I know in here"—she places her hand over her chest—"and in here"—she taps her index finger against her temple—"that no man could ever love them more than he does. He showed me that there are good men out there. He gave me, you, and the girls a family. Something we've been missing outside of the four of us for far too long."

I can't stop the tears as they cascade down my cheeks. "I'm sorry."

"No." Briar's voice is stern. "Don't apologize to me. I agreed to go. If I'm being honest, I wanted to go, but I was intimidated that we wouldn't know anyone there, but I knew that I would have you. I still have you, and you have me, but we have a group of amazing people who have chosen to be our family."

"I don't remember that night. I know you don't either, and I hate that. I hate that I don't know what they did to us. I hate that the girls will one day know and look at us differently. I hate them. I don't know who they are, but I hate them. I don't know what they did," I repeat.

"We're okay," Briar says softly. "We're stronger than the pain. We've come so far since that night."

"I miss Dad," I tell her.

"Me too." Briar smiles through her tears. "He would have loved the men in our lives and our new family. I tell Forrest often that Dad would have loved him and the guys." She turns her eyes to Maddox. "He would have loved you for Brogan."

Maddox shifts beside me, but I don't dare look at him. "Baby." One word, whispered in his broken voice, has me turning my head. His eyes are haunted and glassy, as if he, too, is on the verge of tears. We stare at each other for several long heartbeats before he speaks up.

"I hate them too. I hate that they stole so much from you and your sister. I hate them because they're holding you back from living. I hate them because you're mine, and I can't defend you by kicking their ass," he says, and despite my tears, I smile.

Maddox stands and drops to his knees in front of me. He takes my hands in his, and everything and everyone else fades away. "I can't pretend to know what you're feeling, but I need you to know that I'm here for you. Whatever you need. If you want to cry, scream, fight, whatever you need, I'm your man. Me. I'm the man who wants to stand next to you while you fight the demons of your past. I'm the man who you can depend on. Let me be your pillar of strength until you find the strength that I know lives inside you."

"You still want me?" I ask him.

"Yes. I want you. Today, tomorrow, and every day after. I fall harder for you every single day, and I can't imagine doing life without you."

A sob breaks free from my chest, and my body shakes. "M—Mad—" I can't even say his name because I'm crying so hard.

He sits beside me and lifts me onto his lap, wrapping his arms around me. "I've got you, baby. I've got you," he repeats, holding me tightly. "Together, remember what we said? We're in this together. You and me, we're one unit now. There is no me without you, and we'll get through this. Whatever you need. I'm right here, Brogan."

I don't know how long I cry in his arms, but I do know that something inside me feels lighter. When I've exhausted my tears, I lift my head from his shoulder, and he smiles. His hands lift to gently rest against my cheeks. His thumb traces beneath my eyes. "I want you. I want your past, your present, and your future. For better or worse, right?" He grins.

"I don't remember that either," I tell him.

"Then we renew our vows. You tell me when and where, or I can handle it and tell you when and where. Whatever you need, Brogan. It's yours, as long as it includes me standing next to you."

"You really mean that?"

"I love you, Brogan Lanigan. You've completely stolen my heart, and I'm sorry to tell you, baby, there are no givebacks. Not this time."

I sit up straighter, and his hands fall back to his sides. "Did you just—" I turn to look at my sister. She's crying and smiling, her hands resting over her heart as she watches us. "Did he just—" I can't even say the words. I must not have heard him correctly.

Briar nods, so I turn my eyes to Susan. She's also smiling and nodding. That gives me the courage to look back at Maddox, who's wearing a lazy grin.

"I'm head over heels in love with you. I know you're not there yet, and that's okay, but I need you to know you're not alone. You have me, your sister, and our entire family. We're an off mix, but we're your ride or die until the end."

I'm smiling and the words are on the tip of my tongue, but I can't seem to force them past my lips.

"Brogan?" I turn to face Susan when she speaks. "How do you feel?"

I can't help it; I laugh. "I feel... lighter. I feel lucky to be here. I feel sad because I miss my dad. I feel sad that my decision changed my life and my sister's. I also feel relief. I thought he'd walk away." I pull my eyes back to Maddox. "I was sure you'd see all my broken pieces and bail. I never expected you to be here, and telling me that you love me.... I didn't expect that, or you, Maddox Lanigan."

"Your pieces aren't broken, baby. They're just a little out of order, but we're rearranging them. Together."

I slide off his lap and meet my sister's eyes. "See what I mean? He always knows what to say." I wipe at my eyes.

"Love does that to you. Just ask Forrest, or Roman, or Legend." She grins. "And your husband." She winks at him. "We have a family now who love and support us. I'll always miss Dad, but we have his memory, which will never leave us. He's a part of us in everything that we do. We can miss him, but we can't let the pain keep us from loving again. Missing out on the love that Forrest gives me... I can't imagine a day of my life without him now."

"What she said," Maddox says, reaching over and lacing his fingers through mine.

"I'm proud of you," Susan tells me. "You've made huge strides today, and I'm glad Briar showed up."

"I'll always show up," Briar announces.

"Thank you. All of you. I still have to work through everything bouncing around in my head and in my heart." I squeeze Maddox's fingers to let him know I heard him, and I'm not taking his confession lightly.

"Our time is up for today. Days like today remind me of why I love this job."

"Thank you, Susan."

She nods, and the three of us file out of her office.

"Want to grab something to eat?" I ask Briar.

"Nah, you two go ahead. I'm going home to rescue Roman. He's off today, so he has the girls and Lilly."

I pull my sister into a hug. "Thank you for being here. I love you."

"I love you too."

We ride the elevator back to the first floor and split ways. "Where to?" Maddox asks.

"Do you have work today?"

"No. I moved all of my clients."

"I'm sorry."

"I'm not. There was nothing that could have kept me from being here for you today."

"Let's go home."

"Are you hungry? We can stop and eat or hit a drive-thru."

"Let's just heat up the leftover spaghetti from last night."

"Done." He starts the truck and points it toward home. The one we share together.

For the first time, I allow myself to think about what happens beyond six months. Maddox loves me, and I know that I love him, but something kept me from saying it. I need a little time to process today.

Before I know it, we're pulling into the driveway. "Looks like we got a package," I tell Maddox, seeing the white box leaning against the front door. "Did you order something?"

"Nope. I assumed it was yours."

Exiting the truck, we make our way onto the front porch. Maddox picks up the box and reads the label. "Little White Wedding Chapel." He looks up at me. "Vegas address."

Something an awful lot like fear washes over me. What if there was a mistake? What if we're not really married? It's at this moment, standing on my front porch, that the love I feel for my husband truly hits me.

MADDOX 16

I HOLD THE SMALL WHITE box in my hand as I unlock the door and push it open. I motion for Brogan to go in ahead of me, before stepping in behind her and closing the door. The box, despite its light weight, feels heavy in my hand.

I don't know what it could be, but the thought that we're not really married crosses my mind, and I feel sick at the thought. We move into the living room and sit on the couch.

"I wonder what it is?" Brogan asks. I can tell from her tone of voice she's worried too.

She might not have been able to say the words earlier, but that's okay. I feel her love with every touch, every smile, and every moment of every day. I know she's been through hell and back, and I can wait for her to come to terms with what I already know.

My wife loves me.

"Only one way to find out," I tell her. I offer her the small box, but she shakes her head.

"You do it."

I nod and move to the kitchen to get a knife to cut open the box. It's small, and an odd shape. It doesn't look like it holds paperwork. Maybe we left something at the chapel, and they're sending it to us? I don't remember Brogan mentioning anything that was missing from the trip.

"Here we go." I hold up the knife as I take my seat next to her on the couch. Carefully, I cut at the tape and set the knife on the table in front of us. "Ready?"

"I don't know, but we can't avoid whatever is in there."

Slowly, I open the box and pull out a thumb drive. There's a note card, so I read that aloud. "Congratulations, Mr. and Mrs. Lanigan. Enclosed is your fully edited video of your special day. Thank you for choosing The Little White Wedding Chapel." I drop the note back into the box and stare at the small device in my hands.

"That's a video. Of our wedding," Brogan adds, as if she's trying to process what I just read to her.

"That's what it says." I glance over to see her smiling.

"Can we watch it?" If I'm not mistaken, there is a hint of a smile pulling at her lips.

I swallow hard and nod. I want to watch it, I really do, but something tells me that I was way more into our wedding than what she was. I don't think I forced her or anything, but if she's not smiling and happy, if she looks resigned, I don't know that I'll be able to handle that.

I love her so fucking much.

Standing, I move to the TV and place the thumb drive into the USB slot in the back. Grabbing the remote from the table, I take a seat back on the couch and pat my chest. "I'm gonna need you over here for this." She doesn't argue. She just moves closer and snuggles up to my chest.

My arm wraps around her. I press my lips to the top of her head and hit Play. The logo for the chapel appears, and then the camera is on me. I'm standing at the altar.

"Mr. Lanigan, wave to your bride," the female voice that's recording says.

I wave, with a dopey smile on my face. My eyes are glassy, showing the amount of alcohol we'd consumed that night. "Hey, wifey," I say, my grin growing wider.

"Do you want to say anything for the film?" the lady asks me.

"I can't wait to spend forever with you." I blow the camera a kiss and stand a little taller.

"That was the groom. Let's go check on our bride." She walks down what looks like a hallway and knocks on a door. Brogan must have told her to come in, or someone did, because a few seconds later, she's pushing open the door to step inside.

"Wave to the camera, future Mrs. Lanigan," she tells Brogan.

Brogan waves to the camera. Her eyes are glassy like mine, but her smile is radiant. "Hey, husband." She grins at the camera. "I can't believe you're going to be mine. This is the best day of my life."

"Aww," the woman running the camera says.

The video cuts off and turns back on to recording me standing at the altar. I shift from one foot to the next, but I freeze, and my eyes lock on what I assume is Brogan. They're not showing her on the video, but it has to be my wife who's captured my attention. Eventually, she comes into the frame, and I take her hands in mine.

The video cuts off again. This time it's a new angle, and it points to the doors in the back of the chapel. When they open and Brogan walks through them, she's glowing. She looks happy, and I can tell the moment we lock eyes. Her smile changes. It's a little softer, but the look in her eyes says she's exactly where she wants to be.

She wanted to marry me.

The camera remains on us as the officiant reads us our vows. When it's time for the rings, I pull them out of my pocket, handing one to Brogan, before repeating after the officiant and sliding the ring on her finger. I watch closely for any sign that either one of us don't want this. My hands are steady, and so are hers.

That process is repeated, where she slides my ring onto my finger, and then the famous words pronouncing us husband and wife are declared, and I get to kiss my bride. I watch as my lips move, but I can't make out what I'm saying. Whatever it is, it makes my wife smile.

My eyes are riveted to the screen as I watch myself slide my hand behind her neck and guide her lips to mine. Brogan rises on her toes as I wrap my other arm around her waist and pull her close.

Even on our wedding day, I couldn't get her close enough.

When we come up for air, we're both smiling. I lace her fingers through mine, and we turn to face the videographer. We raise our entwined hands and smile for the camera as we walk down the hall and out of the chapel doors.

The video ends with the logo of the chapel, just as it began. Brogan and I are both quiet, just staring at the screen, and the logo of The Little White Wedding Chapel, the place that changed our lives.

"We looked happy," Brogan says. Her voice is small, but she's cuddled up next to me, so I hear her just fine.

"We did look happy."

She moves to sit up but stays close. Her eyes find mine. "What about now?"

"Am I happy now?" I ask her, and she nods. "I'm not good with words," I tell her, and she scoffs.

"Trust me, you're better than you think you are."

I grab her hand in mine, because I need to be touching her. "I've never felt this kind of happiness. I've never been excited to go to bed because I know I get to hold you. I'm just as excited to wake up with you in my arms. I get your first smiles of the day. I don't remember that." I point toward the screen. "However, I do know that when I woke up in Vegas next to you, wearing this ring, I knew. I knew you were meant to be mine. I felt it in my gut. The entire flight home, all I could think about was how I could convince you to give this a shot. You took a chance on me, and I'm pretty sure I was already halfway in love with you from that alone."

Her smile is soft as she replies, "This kind of happy is new to me too. My entire life, I've felt something missing. I know it was my mom and then my dad. The girls were born at the same time we lost him, and I didn't have time to worry about the missing pieces."

"You didn't have time to find your happy. You were too busy being strong for everyone else."

"Yeah," she agrees, as she moves to climb onto my lap. Once she's straddling me, my hands rest on her thighs as she places a palm on either side of my face. "I wasn't looking for my happy, Maddox. I didn't think I deserved it, and to be honest, there's still a large part of me that still thinks that way. However, today, you didn't even flinch at the appointment with Susan. I was so sure that you were going to walk away from me. That my drama would be too much, but you didn't. Instead, you told me you loved me."

"I do love you, Brogan. Everything I am is yours." I stare into her big green eyes, willing her to believe me. "Your past is not drama; it's your past. It's what helped make you who you are. I know that it takes time for you to truly give your trust and your love, and I'm completely fine with that. I'm here to accept both when you're ready to give them. In the meantime, I want you to know that nothing in your past, your present, or your future will change how I feel about you."

Tears shimmer in her eyes, but the smile that's lighting up her face tells me that this time, they're tears of happiness. Leaning in, she kisses me. I let her set the pace, and she chooses to take her time.

When we finally break apart, there is something shining in her eyes, something that tells me whatever she's about to say is going to rock my world on its axis.

"Maddox Lanigan, I dreamt of you. For months, I would watch you and wish that things could be different. I would dream about what it would be like to be with you. Nothing I ever fantasized about comes close to the real thing. You make me feel strong. You make me feel safe, and there is nothing I love more than having your arms wrapped tightly around me. I look forward to your hugs and your gruff good mornings. I crave your goodnights because I don't get them until I'm wrapped up in your arms." She pauses, but I don't speak, afraid to break her train of thought. "I watched my sister and Forrest, and I always wondered what that would be like. To have a man look at you like you're his lifeline."

My heart is pounding in my chest. This is different. *I* feel different, and by the look in her eyes, she feels this connection. I can see it just as much as I can sense it flowing between us like a live wire.

"Now I know." She smiles, and I don't even think I'm breathing as I wait for her to say more. "I know what it's like to have a good, hardworking, honest man look at you like you hung the moon. I know what it's like to feel safe, loved, and cherished above everything else in his world. You put me at the top of yours. You've allowed me to work through my pain and stood next to me throughout my journey. I have a long way to go, but I'd be lying to us both if I didn't admit that I'm in love with you."

I suck in a sharp breath as my heart expands ten times its size, feeling as though it might burst from my chest. "Say it again." I pull her close to me so there's barely an inch of space between us.

"Maddox Lanigan, I love you."

"Fuck yes, you do." I crash my lips to hers. I put everything I am into this kiss. I need her to know that she's everything. *My* everything.

Her hands grapple between us as she reaches for the hem of my shirt and tugs. "I need this off."

"Yes, ma'am." I smile at her and raise my arms to grab my shirt at the back of my neck and pull it off.

Keeping my hands at my sides, I sit still while hers roam over my chest. I let her explore to her heart's content. It's not until she's reaching for the waistband of my jeans do I speak up.

"Tell me what you want, Brogan." This feels different. She's more open and going for what she wants. I need to make sure I understand before things get out of hand. We've had a major breakthrough and the last thing I want is to scare her, push her too far and set us back with how far we've come.

"I want you."

"You already have me, baby."

"No, I mean, I want you." She pops the button on my jeans.

"Take all the time you need. You don't have to do this because you think I want it, or because you're afraid I'll walk away."

"You've given me time, Maddox. I'm not afraid you'll walk away. Okay, that's a lie. There is still a part of me that worries, but there is a bigger part of me that knows I'm in control. I get to choose something my sister didn't have the luxury to do." She tilts her head to the side, and her tongue peeks out and swipes along her bottom lip. "I choose you, Maddox. For once in my life, I'm turning off the anxiety part of my brain, and I'm following my gut."

"What is your gut telling you?"

"My gut is telling me that I want you to be my first. I want you to make love to me. I want my husband to make love to me."

"I want that, too, baby. However, I feel like I should warn you."

"Warn me?"

I nod. "I've never felt this kind of connection with someone, and I know that if we do this. If we cross that line, I'm never letting you go. I won't be able to do it, Brogan. Already, the thought of us not being together tears me apart from the inside out, but if you were to give me this, and decide you're done, I know for certain I'll never recover."

She's quiet, and I can tell she's processing my words, reading between the lines of what I didn't say. Fuck it, I'm putting it out there. I want zero room for miscommunication. "If we do this, there is no more timeline. No more six months waiting period. I've been dreading every single new day and living for it at the same time. I cherish every day with you, but I dread the time passing so quickly. If we leap over this boundary that has been set between us, I need you to tell me we're forever. No timeline, no 'we're seeing where it goes.' You're my wife, 'til death do us part'." I take a deep breath and ask her one more time, "What about now? What's your gut telling you now?"

"My gut is telling me that I want you to be my first. I want you to make love to me. I want my husband to make love to me. This is forever." She smiles at me, knowing she just repeated her earlier confession word for word.

"I love you, Mrs. Lanigan," I tell her. My heart beats wildly. She's mine. She's finally fucking mine.

"I love you, too, Mr. Lanigan."

"We need to move." I lift her into my arms. She shrieks with laughter as I carry her down the hall to our room. "I need a bed for all the things I want to do to you." When I set her on the bed, she's chewing on her bottom lip. "Hey." I gently tug on that bottom lip with my thumb, getting her to release it. "If at any time you change your mind, you tell me, and we stop."

"Do we need like a word or something?"

"Stop. That's the word. Unless there is a 'don't' in front of it, we stop. It's that simple."

"I know you'll take care of me."

It's not just her words but the honesty I see in her eyes. She believes what she's saying, and that has me wanting to beat on my chest like a caveman. She's mine, all of her, and fuck, I can't wait to show her this next step of how good we are going to be together.

"Always," I assure her. "I'll always take care of you. I'm going to need you to do something for me as well."

"What's that?"

"Strip." Her eyes light up, and that has me feeling ten feet tall and bulletproof. It could also be that I'm about to make love to my wife for the first time.

BROGAN 17

"STRIP," HE SAYS, HIS VOICE commanding yet soft. It's a contradiction, and I can't help but smile, because that's Maddox. He looks like a bad boy at first glance, the kind of man your parents warn you to stay away from. Once you get to know him, you understand that his outward appearance is nothing of who he is inside. His tattoos tell a story of his journey through life, and his heart? Well, it's full of gold. I'm certain of it. He's been so good to me. He's patient, kind, loving, and although I've seen passion from him before, I have a feeling tonight I'm going to get to see a whole new side to my husband, and that excites me just as much as knowing that I'm about to give the man I love a piece of me, that no one else will ever have.

"Brogan?"

Shaking out of my thoughts, I turn my attention back to my husband. "I spaced out for a minute." I smile to let him know I'm okay.

"We don't have to do this."

"Oh, I think we do." I reach for his jeans, and this time, he doesn't stop me. I've already got them unbuttoned, so I ease his zipper down and tug around his waist until I can get them over his hips. He does a little move to get them off his feet and kicks them to the side. Next, I go for his boxer briefs. They're emerald green and do nothing to hide his erection.

Once I get them off him as well, I fist his cock in my hand. He's so close, standing before me as I sit on the bed. He's at the perfect angle for me to do something I've only thought of doing with him.

Moving in, I put him into my mouth. We both moan. I glance up to find his eyes on me.

"You don't have to do this."

I let his hard cock fall from my mouth. "I want to. You tasted me."

"Fuck, baby, I really want you to, if I'm being honest. That hot mouth and those sexy lips wrapped around my cock will be a memory I take to the grave with me, but I'm not coming down your throat, not tonight."

I've never had a man talk to me like this before. Then again, I've never dated, so everything with Maddox is new and exciting. "Then where do you want to... come?" I finally ask, feeling my face heat, but also feeling brazen and bold from his heated stare.

"Inside you."

Heat pools between my thighs. "I'm on the pill," I tell him.

He nods, letting me know he heard me. "I'll wear a condom if you want me to."

"Do you want to?"

"No. I don't want anything between us, but it's not my call to make."

"Is it better without one?" I ask, because what the hell do I know?

"I don't know."

"What do you mean, you don't know?"

"I've never had sex without one."

"But you want to with me?" I know I sound like a teenager right now, but I have zero experience with this. Sure, Briar and I, and even the girls, have had talks, but no amount of girl talk prepared me for my husband standing before me, telling me he wants nothing between us.

"You're my wife, Brogan. I never want anything to come between us, whether that be a thin layer of latex on my cock, or any other outside distraction that could potentially take you away from me. I saved this for you. I know it's not the same as what you're giving me, but I, too, have never trusted someone to not try to get pregnant on purpose, so I made sure I always supplied the protection, even if they had it, we used mine. Fuck," he says, tilting his head back. "I hate talking about my past with you while you're staring at my cock like it's your next meal."

"I was kinda hoping it would be," I say, shrugging.

"Tell me what you want, Brogan, and it's yours."

"What if I get pregnant? I mean, nothing is one-hundred-percent, right?"

"Then we start our family."

Tears burn, but I blink them away. "Just like that?"

"Yeah, baby, just like that."

I want that. I want him and the life he keeps saying that we can have together. "Okay. Then we don't use one."

"You sure?"

"I want something of yours that no one else has."

"Baby, you have my heart. That's only ever going to be yours. We can wait on this one."

"I don't want to wait. No more waiting, right? That's what you said. That if we do this, if we take this step, then it's us forever."

"That's what I said."

"Then let's start our forever." Five words. That's all it takes for me to seal our fate, for me to accept that this is real. That Maddox is my husband, and not because we got married when we were drunk in Vegas, but because he chose me.

Every single day, this amazing man chooses me.

I choose him too.

Bending, he captures my lips in a kiss that I'm certain would make my knees weak if I were not sitting. When he finally pulls away, he's all business. "I need you naked." Stepping back, he offers me his hand and helps me stand.

I expect him to help me get undressed, so I'm surprised when he climbs into bed in all of his naked glory and places his hands behind his head as he watches my every move.

"You're not going to help me?" I ask him.

"Nope."

There's something about his heated gaze as it washes over me that gives me the courage I need to strip for him. Not just take off my clothes, but I do it slowly, swaying my hips, and putting on a show for him.

By the time I'm finished, he's stroking his cock, and his eyes burn with desire. "Come here, baby."

I do as he says and climb on the bed. Despite not having any clothes on, I'm not cold. My body is feverish with how much I want him. I start to settle beside him, but he grabs my hips and moves me to straddle him. His hard length rests just below where I need him to be, so when I rock my hips, his cock rubs against my clit. I moan at the contact.

"I thought maybe you might want to take control. You take as little or as much as you need."

My face heats, but I don't let that keep me from telling him what I want. If I've learned anything about my husband, it's that I can say anything, and he's still going to be here. My heart knows that, and my head, well, it's starting to get on board with that realization. I'm certain I'll have days where I have setbacks, but tonight, that worry is pushed to the side.

"I don't want to be in control. Not tonight. Not this time. I feel like so much of our time together has been me trying to steer us to something that was inevitable. My head tried to convince me we'd never be here, but my heart knew better. Tonight, I just want to feel. I don't want to have to think or make any more choices. Tonight, I want to be your wife, and I want my husband to have his wicked way with me."

His cock twitches as a slow, sexy grin tilts his lips. "Not just tonight, baby. Every night, for forever, you are my wife." He grips my hips, and before I know what's happening, he's flipped us, so I'm on my back and he's hovering over me.

I widen my legs, making room for him, and he settles between them, exactly where he's meant to be. Not sure where to put my hands, I rest them against either side of his face, cupping his cheeks. "I love you, Maddox."

"I love you too, Brogan." He drops his elbow to the bed, shifting all his weight to the left side, while his right hand ventures between us. "I need to make sure you're ready."

I laugh at that. "I'm ready, trust me."

"I don't want to hurt you."

"It's supposed to hurt the first time, right?"

"Yeah, but I don't want it to."

"I trust you." As I say the words, I feel them cement themselves in my mind.

"Just let me make sure." He slides his fingers through my folds and hisses. "Fuck, wet silk. That's what I'm feeling right now."

He slides one long thick digit inside me, and I lift my hips, needing more. His lips find mine in a kiss so sensual, I feel like I could combust just from his mouth on mine. However, my husband has other plans. He adds another finger, and I moan because it feels good. Too good.

"You, Maddox. I want you."

"You have me."

"In-Inside me," I pant. "Please. I've waited so long."

That's all it takes for him to remove his fingers and bring them to his mouth. He sucks them clean, then smirks as he kisses me again. I can taste myself on his tongue, and that makes me even hotter. I've imagined this so many times, but my imagination has nothing on the real thing.

With his hands braced on either side of my head, he pushes forward. I tense up when I feel him, and he freezes.

"Don't stop. Why did you stop?" I ask him.

"You tensed."

"Don't stop." I lift my hips, and he slides in a little further. "I want all of you."

"I don't want to hurt you."

"You'll make it better."

"Every day, baby." He slides in a little at a time, giving me time to adjust with each push of his hips.

"Just do it, Maddox."

He nods and thrusts forward, and I feel a pinch of pain, but nothing at all like I was expecting. He bends and buries his face in my neck. His heavy breaths fall against my neck as I bury my nails in the exposed skin of his back.

"I'm okay," I tell him.

"I just need a second," he tells me.

"I promise you, I'm okay. You can move."

He lifts his head, and his blue eyes, filled with so much love, stare down at me. "I've never felt anything like this, Brogan. I don't know if it's because there's no barrier between us or because I love you so fucking much, but this… it's like nothing ever before, and if I move right now, I'm going to lose control, and this is going to be over far too soon."

"That's okay, we have forever, right?" I ask, smiling up at him. My tone is light, and I feel like a weight has been lifted from my shoulders. It doesn't matter how fast this is over, because we have the rest of our lives to repeat this night.

He huffs out a laugh. "That is most certainly not okay. You come first. Always."

"What kind of rule is that?" I ask him, smiling at the way he's always taking care of me.

"It's my rule. It should be every man's rule." He slowly pulls out and pushes back in. "You feel incredible wrapped around me. So hot and wet. I could live here, inside you, for the rest of my life."

"Well, how about unlimited access the rest of your life? We still have jobs and families we have to see," I tease him.

"There is no one else but you. You're all I see, all I feel," he says, pushing back in. He's finding a rhythm, and I love every second of it.

I want him closer. I need—I don't really know what, but I know that I need something. Wrapping my legs around his waist, I hold on tightly, and he slides deeper.

"Fuck," he rasps, as he continues to pump in and out of me. "Touch yourself."

"What?"

"Slide your hand down to your pussy, and rub your clit. I need you to come because I don't know how much longer I'm going to be able to hold on."

Too turned on to care about what he's asking me to do, I slide my hand between us and rub on my clit. Instantly, I moan at the contact. I'm so sensitive.

"There you go," he praises. "Good girl. Keep going. I need you to come for me, Brogan."

It's as if his words have a direct line to my pleasure, because I feel it building. "Mad—" I try to say his name, but the feeling is too much. The fire of my orgasm builds as it rushes to my core. When it finally hits like a tsunami, I call out for him.

"That's it, there's my girl," he says, pumping faster. "Fuck, you're sexy. Your pussy is going crazy, baby." He grits his teeth, and I feel the moment he releases inside me. Pulse after pulse until we're both spent. Maddox somehow manages to flip us both over so I'm lying on top of him without losing contact.

He's still buried inside me as I rest my head on his chest, feeling the rapid rise and fall as he labors for each breath.

"You doing okay?" he asks, kissing the top of my head.

I lift so that I can see him. "When can we do that again?" I ask, and he sputters with laughter. I find myself smiling at his reaction, even though I was deadly serious.

"You're going to be sore," he tells me, his breathing more even now.

"Worth it," I say, and his body shakes as he laughs.

"Come on, wife. We're all sweaty and messy. We need a shower."

I climb off him, missing the connection, and he's right. We're messy, and we definitely need a shower. He follows me into the bathroom and turns on the water. As it's warming, he lifts me into his arms, and I lock my arms and legs around him, accepting his kiss.

"I love you, Mrs. Lanigan." His eyes are bright, and he looks happy.

He looks as happy as I feel, and I need him to know that, so I return his smile. "I love you too, Mr. Lanigan."

"Why did we agree to do this again?" Maddox asks. He's standing behind me while I try to finish getting ready. He trails his lips down my neck, distracting me.

"Because they're our family, and we've been married for over five months and we have yet to host family dinner."

"I want you to be my dinner."

"Stop." I laugh. "You are not going to get me all worked up before everyone gets here."

"We have time."

"They'll be here in ten minutes."

"I can be quick."

"We both know that's not true." It's been two weeks since we first slept together, and I've lost count of how many times since. We can't keep our hands off each other, and it's been... glorious.

"Fine, but I get to tell them you're mine."

"I'm pretty sure they already know." Briar swears they could all see through our "we're giving it six months" mantra.

"Don't care. I'm telling them."

"Are you going to keep your hands to yourself today?"

"What? No. Why in the hell would I do that?"

"Because the kids will be there."

"Baby, those kids have seen it already. If you think for a second, Roman, Legend, or Forrest keep their hands off their wives because their kids are around, you're wrong. Besides, it's good for them to see strong, healthy, loving relationships."

"Well, aren't you insightful today?"

"Nah, I saw it on TV, one of those talk show things Lyra likes to watch at the shop."

I burst out laughing just as we hear someone call out to us. "Go. Greet them. I have to put my earrings in and I'll be right there."

"Fine. Love you."

My heart melts for him. I'll never get tired of hearing him tell me that he loves me. "I love you too." I peck a kiss to his lips. "Now go." I push at him playfully, and he backs away, hands raised, winks, and walks out the door to greet our family.

"There she is," Maddox says as I enter the living room. The gang is already here. I make my way to where he's sitting, and he pulls me onto his lap. "Did you hear the good news?" Maddox asks the room.

"Are you having a baby too?" Rayne asks.

Briar freezes as her eyes find mine.

"You're pregnant?" I ask.

She nods with tears in her eyes. "We told the girls first. We were going to tell everyone today. We just found out yesterday."

"Briar." My voice cracks, and tears fill my eyes. I stand, and so does she, and we meet in the middle of my living room to hug. We're both crying, and when I feel arms wrap around me, I see it's Maggie, Monroe, and Emerson.

The five of us stand huddled together, all crying because of this beautiful moment. My sister didn't have anyone but me and our dad when she found out about her first pregnancy. Despite all she went through, she loved her babies, and now, here we are, both married to incredible men, and she's doing it again. This time with the father by her side, every step of the way.

Finally, we break our little huddle and go back to our seats. "Are you?" River asks, and I laugh.

"No, sweetie, I'm not having a baby."

"We could," Maddox whispers, and as always, my husband knows what to say to claim another broken piece of my heart as his.

"We're married," Maddox tells the girls.

"We knowed that, Uncle Maddox," Rayne replies.

"Yeah, but this time, it's different," he says, trying to explain it to my nieces.

"How?" River asks.

"Well—" Maddox starts, and I jump in to save him.

"It's not different," I tell them. "It's better. We're just really happy, and we wanted to tell you all about that." The adults in the room are able to read between the lines. The ladies smile with happy tears glistening in their eyes. Whether that's from our announcement or Briar's, I'm not sure. Probably both, and the guys, they're all smiling and nodding, wearing smug expressions. Yeah, I know, I was late to the game, but I'm here now, and I'm ready to take in everything it entails.

The twins seem to accept my answer as they rush to the corner where we keep toys for them and start to play. Lilly chases after them while Kane sleeps peacefully in his daddy's arms. Maddox wraps his arms around me and rests his chin on my shoulder while Roman tells him about his client yesterday. Everyone is laughing and talking, and happy.

Me most of all.

I never knew I could have this. I'm so thankful for this life and what's yet to come. I'd like to think our dad had a hand in guiding us here. Maybe it was Mom too. They're together now, and I know they'd want nothing more than for Briar and me to be happy and settled.

We've found our tribe, our people, our family.

"Let's eat," Maddox says, pulling me out of my thoughts.

With a flurry of activity, we all find our way to the kitchen to make our plates, and I can't help but think back to the day a little over a year ago when everyone was here for the twins' fourth birthday. So much has changed since then, but I wouldn't change a single second of any of it.

MADDOX 18

IT'S MY WIFE'S BIRTHDAY WEEK. It's a week of celebrating I can get behind with all that I am, because we get to celebrate her. Not just my wife, but my sister-in-law, Briar, too.

Forrest and I have been planning this celebration for weeks now. At first we talked about a kid-free night out with just the adults, but we immediately vetoed that idea. Briar and Brogan would want the girls there, and all the kids, actually. They're all about family and being together and after all that they've lost, we understand that.

So, we enlisted the help of Legend, Roman, and Lachlan, and an idea was born. It was Roman who suggested we reach out to Royce Riggins, a long-time client. He and his family have a huge cabin in Gatlinburg that they let friends and family use if they're not using it. One phone call and we were booked for this weekend, Thursday through Sunday.

"You're really not going to tell me where we're going?" Brogan asks from the passenger seat of my truck.

"Nope," I say, grinning. The guys and I decided this would be a surprise for not just Brogan and Briar, but for Monroe and

Emerson too. We did tell Maggie but swore her to secrecy. We knew the ladies would want her there, and well, she doesn't have a husband who can tell her to pack a bag and ask off work for a few days. Lachlan is picking her up, so she doesn't have to drive by herself, and the rest of us, well, we're taking our families on a trip, and our wives have no idea.

We had to say there's a "no cell" phone rule for the weekend. It's a lie. We'll give them back to them as soon as we get to the cabin, but it was too risky that they would text each other and figure us out.

"Why do you get your phone, and I don't get mine?" Brogan asks.

"Because I need it for the GPS."

She pouts in the passenger seat, looking cute as hell. "I'm not good with surprises, Maddox."

I reach over and place my hand on her thigh. "I know, baby, but I promise you this is going to be a good surprise. I just wanted to do something special for you for your birthday."

"But I always spend my birthday with Briar."

"I know, but please, can we have this weekend?" I feel like an asshole not telling her. I have to keep reminding myself that the surprise will be worth it.

"Yeah," she finally agrees. "I guess this year is different for both of us. We both have husbands now."

"That's the spirit." If we pull this off, it's going to be epic.

Three and a half hours later, we're pulling into the cabin. We're the last to arrive from the looks of the four other trucks parked outside. Brogan gasps as she recognizes the trucks.

"They're all here?" she asks.

"Yes."

"Maddox!" She turns to me, and she's smiling.

"I'd never take you away from your sister on your birthday."

"I love you."

"And I love you. Come on. Let's go inside. I'll get our bags later." I don't bother to tell her to wait for me to get her door, because I know she's too excited for that. She hops out of the truck, and I do the same, lacing my fingers with hers as we take each step to the front porch. On the final step, the door bursts open, and Briar comes rushing out. I drop Brogan's hand just in time for her twin sister to launch herself into my wife's arms.

"Can you believe this?" Briar asks. "You have to see the cabin. This place is insane."

Brogan looks back at me over her shoulder where I stand watching my wife and her sister have their moment. "Go check it out. I'll get our bags." That's the only encouragement she needs as they rush inside to check the place out.

I take my time getting back to the truck, grabbing both of our bags, and heading inside.

"Hey," Forrest greets me with a one-armed hug. "There are a million bedrooms left to choose from."

I laugh at that. "I'll let Brogan choose," I say, placing our bags on the floor. I whistle when I take in the cabin. It's not overly fancy, but it's exactly what a cabin in the Smoky Mountains should be. Lots of windows looking over the vast mountains, and a huge living space big enough to support a large family.

"Good thing Royce is giving us the family discount on this place. I don't know if we could have afforded it otherwise," Lachlan says.

"I had to force him to do that," Roman speaks up. "He wanted to give it to us for free, and said he'd be by the new shop for some more ink, but I insisted."

"Thanks for doing this," I tell him.

"The ladies are happy." Roman nods.

"They are."

The five of us, along with the twins, Lilly, and Kane, settle in the living room. The kids have already got toys spread out to play with, and it makes me smile. I can't wait until this is our home, full of toys and the pitter-patter of little feet. Some parents complain about stepping over toys, and I can't wait for it. I can't wait to start a family with my wife.

A few hours later, the guys and I are in the kitchen making dinner. We've vowed that our wives, and Maggie, of course, have a nice relaxing weekend, and we're going to take care of everything.

"Thanks for being born," Monroe tells them. "I can get behind being spoiled like this." She laughs.

"It's nice," Emerson agrees, "but I also like to be the one spoiling. I feel like Rome does so much for Lilly and me already."

"For sure," Monroe agrees.

"Right?" Briar says. "I don't know how we got so lucky."

"We're the lucky ones," I call out to them, and they all laugh.

"You're not supposed to be listening to us!" Brogan calls back.

"You know better than that," I say, joining them at the table and placing a bottle of water in front of her. "Anyone else need a drink?" I ask. They call off what they'd like, and I move back to the kitchen to get it, but Lachlan is already pulling the drinks out of the fridge and moving to pass them out.

"Ladies." He winks.

"Don't flirt with my wife!" Roman, Forrest, Legend, and I all shout at the exact same time. The ladies snicker, and Lachlan smirks.

"I can't help it. It's my sex appeal. Chicks dig it," he jokes.

I turn to glare at him, but find him grinning and tossing a wink at Maggie. Her face heats, but she quickly looks away as if nothing happened. Interesting. I make a mental note to ask Brogan if she noticed that little display later tonight.

Once dinner is ready, we rally the troops and sit down at the huge dining table together to eat. We laugh, we talk, and enjoy a great meal. For the next couple of hours, we play with the kids, and once they go to bed, we build a fire in the fireplace, and we're all snuggled up. The ladies, minus Briar, have a glass of wine, while the guys all have a beer, well, all except for Forrest. In solidarity with his wife, he's not drinking. I imagine I'll be the same way once Brogan is pregnant. Not to mention I'm certain I'll be a mess and will want to stay sober in case she needs anything.

"What are you thinking about?" Brogan asks.

"How when we're pregnant, I'll probably not drink like Forrest tonight, because I'll want to make sure I have my wits about me if there is anything that you need."

"I wouldn't expect you to do that," she tells me.

"I know, and that only makes me want to do it even more." I kiss her cheek.

"When are you thinking that this might happen?" she asks, keeping her voice low as she takes a sip of her wine.

"What about now?" I ask her, and her body shakes with silent laughter.

"Maybe not tonight." She raises her glass of wine to remind me she's been drinking. "We could practice."

"Now?"

She chuckles softly. "Later. But you'll have to be quiet."

"Me? You're the one who can't be quiet."

"Well, we're both going to have to if we want to practice here."

"We'll make it work," I assure her, kissing her neck.

"Briar, are you going to find out what you're having?" Maggie asks. She's sitting on the love seat with her feet propped up on Lachlan's lap.

"I think so. We want to be able to decorate the nursery and be prepared. I got rid of everything from when the girls were babies. I never thought I'd be here."

"Oh, we'll throw you a shower," Monroe tells her.

"You're not supposed to with second pregnancies, though, right?" Briar asks.

Monroe waves her hand in the air. "Who cares what society says? It's been five years and you're going to need all the things, and we are more than happy to assist you with that."

"What she said," Emerson chimes in.

The ladies start chatting about baby showers, and things Forrest and Briar will need, while the guys, well, we're content just to listen to them be happy.

Three bottles of wine later, the ladies are ready for bed. As we stand, Brogan speaks up. "Thank you." Her voice cracks, but I'm not sure anyone notices but me. I'm sure Briar hears it, too, but as for the rest of them, I doubt they can tell she's emotional.

"Thank you for being the amazing humans you are. For bringing us into your lives, and embracing all of us so freely. I just wanted to tell you that I'm honored to be a part of this group."

"Family," Roman reminds her. "You're a part of our family."

She nods and offers him a watery smile. "Family," she repeats.

"I'll see you all in the morning. My wife and I have some practicing to do." Laughter follows us up the stairs. No other explanation needed because I know damn good and well the rest of them are going to be doing the same thing. Maybe even Lachlan and Maggie, if the looks they've been giving each other all night are any indication.

I carry my wife to our room and pull open the curtains. The moonlight shines down over the mountains and gives a soft glow into the room. I take my time stripping her out of her clothes before we climb under the covers. We need to be quiet, so I slow things down and make sweet love to her before we both fall into a sated, exhausted sleep.

<hr />

"Are we not going home?" Brogan asks as I drive past our road.

"No. We have one more stop to make."

"Another surprise?"

"Dinner with my parents," I tell her. What I don't tell her is that Forrest, Briar, and the girls will also be there. My mom insisted that she make Brogan a birthday dinner, and that her sister and nieces be there as well. I believe her exact words were, "Maddox, she should have her entire family there." Which led to me telling her she better be ready to feed an army because her entire family was a lot bigger than just Forrest, Briar, and the girls. Eventually we settled on just us for this time around so that Mom and Dad could get to know Brogan, Briar, River, and Rayne better.

As I pull into my parents' driveway, I park the truck. We beat Forrest, and I'm glad. That just sweetens the surprise she has no idea is coming. Today is their official twenty-fourth birthday, and I'm certain my mom has pulled out all the stops.

Hand in hand, we make our way inside. "Mom, Dad, where are you?" I call out, mainly to let them know we're here. Trust me, my parents have been caught in compromising positions over the years that I do not want to think about or subject my wife to on her birthday.

"Happy Birthday!" Mom steps around the island and pulls Brogan into a big hug before moving to the side and making room for my dad to do the same.

"Thank you." Brogan smiles at them. "Can I help?"

Mom gasps. "On your birthday? No, ma'am, you take a seat. Maddox, get your wife a drink."

"Yes, ma'am." I let my hand trail over Brogan's ass as I move around her to the refrigerator.

"This looks amazing. Thank you so much for making dinner," Brogan tells my mom.

"It's not much, just spaghetti and meatballs, but a little birdie might have told me that you love Italian."

"I do," Brogan tells her.

The doorbell chimes, and voices ring out right after. Voices that I know she recognizes by the look on her face. I don't get time to tell her what's going on before Forrest, Briar, and the girls step into the kitchen.

"Aunt Brogan!" River cheers.

"Uncle Maddox!" Rayne says excitedly.

"We missed you," they say at the same time.

"I missed you too." I bend down to wrap them both in a hug.

"What are you doing here?"

"We're celebrating your birthday," my mom tells her. "We couldn't do that without your sister."

I look up at Brogan and there are tears in her eyes. "Really?" She can see for herself that they're here, but she's so overcome with emotion, she asks just to make sure.

"Really," Mom says, coming to stand next to her and pulling her into a hug. Her voice is quiet, but we all hear her when she says, "I know your parents aren't here to celebrate with you, and well, I know that we can never fill their shoes, but we'd like to be placeholders for them if you'll have us." She glances over at Briar and holds out her hand. My sister-in-law doesn't hesitate to take it. The three of them are in a small huddle, now whispering words I can't make out, but they're all smiling with tears in their eyes.

Happy tears.

"Who are you?" River asks, always the inquisitive one.

"My name is Cassie. I'm Maddox's mommy."

"Oh," she and Rayne reply at the same time.

"But you can call me Grandma."

"Really? We don't have one of those here. Our grandma is in heaven," Rayne explains.

There are very few things in life that get me in my feels, but this right here, I'm feeling it. I know I've been telling Brogan this from the very beginning, but it's finally setting in for me. We are their only family. Instead of holding my wife, I wrap my arm around my mom and kiss her cheek. No words are said, but none are needed. She knows what she's offering and how much it means to me. She knows how much it means to them.

"I'm Hank," my dad speaks up. "But I was kind of hoping you'd call me Grandpa."

"We don't gots one of those either," River says, with excitement in her eyes.

"Ours is with our grandma in heaven," Rayne explains, sounding far older than her five years of age.

"That's our mommy and daddy." River points to Forrest and Briar.

"Our mommy has a baby in her belly," Rayne says cheerily.

"I've known your daddy since he was your age," my dad tells them.

"You did?" they ask at the same time.

"We sure did. Now, I need some help. I made a big ol' pot of spaghetti and meatballs. Do you girls think you could help me eat it?"

"Oh, we love sketti." Rayne smiles up at my mom, and I can see her heart melt for my nieces.

"Perfect. And guess what?" Mom's pretending to be whispering, but we can all hear her.

"What?" the girls ask, whisper shouting and leaning in toward my mom.

"After dinner, we get to have cake and ice cream."

"Is it a birthday cake?" River asks.

"Yes. Homemade."

"What's that mean?" Rayne asks.

"It means that I made it right here in my kitchen instead of buying it from the store or bakery."

"Oh, we like to bake too. Uncle Maddox and Aunt Brogan let us bake cookies when we had a sleepover."

"They did?" Mom sounds shocked, playing into their responses. "Well, I wonder if sometime you could have a sleepover here and we can bake all the goodies."

"Mommy, can we?" River asks.

"Please, can we?" Rayne adds.

"I'm sure we can make that happen," Briar tells them.

"Dinner is ready. Let's eat," Hank calls out.

Forrest and I help make plates for the girls and set them at the table between us. Brogan and Briar sit together on the opposite side of the table, and my parents are at either end.

The day is filled with laughter, love, and family. When my eyes meet my wife's across the table, she mouths, "I love you," and I give her words right back to her. This is our life now, and what our future will look like for many years to come.

I can't wait to see what happens next.

Tonight feels like old times, only better. It's better because instead of sitting in Forrest's backyard around the fire holding my beer, I'm holding my wife and my beer. I'm pretty damn sure it doesn't get better than that. Oh wait, it does because my wife is in love with me. The night couldn't be more perfect.

Somehow, after dinner last night at my parents' place for Briar and Brogan's birthdays, we ended up with my parents offering to watch the girls, which led to Monroe calling her parents to watch Kane, and Roman calling his to watch Lilly, and here we are, having an adult night.

Brogan snuggles close to me, and I wrap my arms a little tighter around her waist. "Love you," I whisper, keeping my words soft just for her. She turns her head to smile at me, and I lean in for a quick kiss. Just a peck on her lips, but it's perfect.

"It's so weird with the kids not being here," Forrest speaks up.

"It is, but it's also nice to know they're safe and that we can unwind a little," Monroe says.

"You want to unwind with me, baby?" Legend asks her.

"Later." She winks, and Legend pulls her into a kiss so heated, I'm sure someone flying overhead in a plane would feel uncomfortable watching them.

"I agree," Emerson adds. "I love my daughter, but it's nice to have a night just to be us, how it all started."

"Might be a good time to give Lilly a little brother or sister." Monroe winks at her best friend.

"Now *that* I can get behind. What do you think, baby girl?" Roman asks his wife. "Time to head home?"

"No." Emerson chuckles. "It's not time to go home, but if you're not too tired, we can probably make time when we get home."

"La la la la la," Forrest sings loudly. "I love you both, I do, but, dude, she's my sister," Forrest complains good-naturedly.

"She's my wife," Roman counters. "You're going to have to get past it."

"Leave them alone," Briar tells her husband, and he instantly turns all his focus to her. Even with nothing but the light of the fire, I can see his entire demeanor change. He softens for her, just as he does with their daughters.

"Baby, she's my little sister."

"And he's your best friend, her husband, and the father of your niece. It's been years, Forrest. You know she's in good hands," Briar reminds him.

"Oh, she's in expert hands, all right," Roman quips.

Forrest groans, and everyone else laughs at their antics. We all know Forrest has accepted the two of them and that he knows how much Roman loves Emerson. He's just playing, and the twitch of his lips as he's also trying not to laugh is a testament to that.

"At least with the kids here, I have someone to snuggle," Maggie quips.

"Aww, Mags, you need me to snuggle you?" Lachlan asks her.

Maggie crosses her eyes and sticks her tongue out at him, and we all snicker.

"How are you feeling?" Emerson asks Briar.

"Good. Really good." Her eyes meet Forrest's, and I swear his smile lights up the night sky.

Not that I can blame him. If my wife were pregnant, I'd be beaming too. Speaking of. "When can we do that?" I whisper to Brogan.

"Do what?" she whispers back.

"Have a baby." I slide my hands under her shirt and rest them protectively on her belly. Fuck me, the thought of my wife growing a part of us is an aphrodisiac.

She sits up from where she was leaning against my chest so that her eyes are level with mine. "A baby?" Shock is written all over her face.

Keeping one hand on her belly beneath her shirt, I raise the other to rest against her cheek. "Yeah, we both want a family." I pause. Has she changed her mind? "That's still what you want, right? To have a family? With me?" Even I can hear the worry in my tone, and if this woman sitting on my lap didn't mean the world to me, I might feel a little ashamed of the fear that's simmering in my veins.

"I want a family."

I swallow hard. She wants a family, just not with me. That's a kick to the gut that I wasn't expecting.

"With you," she says, leaning in close. "Only with you. I could never imagine being... intimate like that with anyone but you. I know you'd never hurt me, Maddox."

Fear instantly fades to my heart, throwing a rager in my chest. "Never. I only want to love you, Brogan."

"So, you're ready? To have a baby?"

I nod. "When you are. You tell me when." I slide my hand behind her neck and pull her lips to mine. "In the meantime," I murmur, "we should practice."

"You know we can hear you, right?" Lachlan asks.

Brogan giggles, burying her face in my chest. "Then you heard me and the love of my life, my wife, Mrs. Lanigan, discussing when we're ready to add to the Everlasting Ink family."

"Well, hurry it up," Lachlan tells us. "We need one more, so we don't have to fight over the ones we have now."

"Hey, we're almost there," Forrest speaks up.

"Babe, I'm barely pregnant." Briar laughs.

"Yeah, but the deed is done. We're ahead of all of them," Forrest reminds her.

"Baby girl, you hear that?" Roman asks. "Are we going to let them win?"

"Well, first of all, they already have us by one, and one on the way, so yeah, I think we are." Emerson snickers.

"What if you have twins?" Monroe asks.

"I think if anyone is having twins, it's us," Brogan speaks up, and immediately slaps her hand over her mouth.

I hug her tighter, because my fucking wife, she's a fighter, and it's so damn good to see her living this life with me, and not fearing what-ifs. "Yeah," I say, backing her up.

"What if *we're* having twins?" Forrest asks.

Brogan gasps. "Are you?"

"No." Briar shakes her head. "Not that we're aware of."

"I need to call my parents," Legend says, playing with Monroe's hair where she sits in his lap.

"Why?" Monroe asks him.

"To see if there is a long-lost chance that twins run in our family. We can't let them win, baby."

We all crack up laughing, and a rightness I've never felt washes over me. I love my friends and their wives, but having mine here makes nights like these even sweeter.

BROGAN 19

SIX MONTHS AGO TODAY, I woke up in Vegas realizing that I was married. Married to a man who I'd wanted from afar but was too afraid to tell him. It was more than just the fear. It was me not thinking I was worthy enough to have him in my life as more than just one of my brother-in-law's best friends.

Six months ago, Maddox asked me to give him a shot. To give him six months to prove to me what he claimed he already knew.

That we belonged together.

So much has changed in those twenty-six weeks. I've changed. Some might say it was the therapy, which I know was part of it, but I also know I never could have seen the growth that I have without my husband.

He's the greatest man I've ever known, and no matter what hurdle we faced, he was next to me, cheering me on, telling me that we've got this.

One hundred and eighty-two days ago, I didn't believe him. I never thought we would be here, but we are. I still have moments where I'm insecure about deserving this much happiness, but Maddox is always right there to remind me that I am.

And I believe him.

I believe in his love.

I believe in my love for him.

I believe in us.

The patio door opens, and Maddox walks out. He's in a pair of khaki cargo shorts and a tight-fitting Everlasting Ink T-shirt. It's summer in Tennessee, and the weather is beautiful, so we decided to have dinner out here tonight.

"Are you ready for me to toss the steaks on the grill?" he asks.

"I'm still full from lunch."

He nods. "Me too. That pan crust is filling," he says, of the large meat lover's pizza we had from Dough Daddies on our way home from the grocery store. We've settled into a routine, as an old married couple, if you will, and I love it.

"What's bringing that gorgeous smile to your face?" Maddox asks. I scoot over on the double lounger to make room for him to join me.

"I was just thinking about how we have a routine. If neither one of us works, we do our grocery shopping on Saturdays, and clean on Sundays."

"We're very domesticated," he says, laughing. "I love our routine."

"I do too. I was just thinking we're an old married couple already."

"It's fucking perfect," he says, wrapping his arms around me as I settle on his chest. "I love it here."

"Yeah?"

He nods. "I always loved this house."

"So, you think this is where we're going to stay?"

"Do you not want to?"

"No, I do, but I wasn't sure what you wanted."

"Baby, we could live anywhere. You are what makes it a home. The love we share, but this is your family home, and I just assumed this is where we would settle. We can do some updating, and over there is the perfect spot for a swing set." He points to the corner of the yard. "It's in perfect view of the window over the sink to watch the kids play."

"Yeah, and maybe we could update the primary bathroom," I say, thinking about our shower habits. It's nice that we're forced to be so close since we usually can't keep our hands off each other, but a little more room would be nice too.

"We can do that. There's a lot of open space not being used in the current layout."

"What about you? Anything you'd like to change?"

"Maybe build a garage that my truck will fit in," he says, laughing.

"What about your house?"

"I say we put it on the market, unless you want to live there."

"It's small," I say, wrinkling my nose. "I can't see us raising kids there."

He nods. "I'll call the realtor tomorrow."

"Will it always be like this?"

"Like what?"

"You agreeing with everything that I say or suggest."

"I'm sure there will be times we disagree. When that day comes, we'll talk it out. But I'm an easygoing guy for the most part. I need you, and when we have kids, I'll need them. I want my friends who are my brothers to always be involved. My parents, too, and other than that, I don't care. I don't care where we are, whose house we invade, or what we have to eat while doing it. That's all just noise."

"You know, I think maybe my dad has a little something to do with us meeting."

"Yeah?"

I nod. "He loved this place. His parents loved this place, and Briar and I always looked forward to visiting here when we were growing up. When we lost him, and had to sell the house in Nashville, we both just knew this is where we would go. Moving here helped us feel closer to him being in one of his favorite places. We liked the slower pace of small-town life versus the busy streets of Nashville. Dad made sure this place was in our names and we didn't even know he did it."

"So not just fate, my father-in-law had something to do with it." He tilts his head back and looks up at the evening sky as the sun starts to fade. "Mr. and Mrs. Pearce, my name is Maddox Lanigan, and I'm in love with your daughter. Six months ago, she married me, and there hasn't been a single day since that I've not thanked God for her coming into my life."

"Maddox." I place my hand over my mouth to keep my sobs from breaking free.

"My wife tells me that you two might have had something to do with us meeting. You specifically, Mr. Pearce, and I'd like to say thank you. Thank you for bringing me the love of my life."

He peers down at me and smiles. "I love her. Brogan is my entire world, and from all the stories she's told me, we would have gotten along really well." He kisses my temple and looks back up at the sky. "That's good, because I have a question to ask you. Sir, I'd love your permission to marry your daughter. I know what you're thinking, that we're already married, and that's true, but she didn't get the wedding of her dreams, and I want to give her that. Whatever that day looks like, she'll have it."

I'm openly sobbing, but he doesn't stop staring up at the sky, but he does tighten his hold on me.

"I know you can't answer me, but I wanted to ask you all the same. I love her with every fiber of my being, and I promise to love her for all the days of my life." He stands and offers me his hand. I place mine in his and allow him to help me stand as well. I don't know where we're going or what we're doing, but I'd follow this man anywhere.

Maddox kisses the corner of my mouth, then drops to one knee. "Brogan Lanigan, you are my sun and my stars. You're my everything. My wife. My best friend. Will you do me the incredible honor of spending your life with me? Baby, will you marry me? Again?" he asks, smiling up at me.

Reaching into his pocket, he pulls out the most beautiful diamond engagement ring I've ever seen. It's shaped like a heart, with a band of diamonds on either side. "You're my heart, Brogan. You own every piece of me."

"I don't want another wedding." His face falls, so I'm quick to keep talking. "I don't remember the first one, but we have the video, and we looked really happy that day, Maddox. It might have taken alcohol to get us to take the first step, but I'm glad we took it." I wipe at my cheeks as he stands with his hands still holding mine. "That's our story, and I don't want to erase it." I hold my left hand out to him, and he doesn't waste a single second to slide the diamond on my finger right next to the diamond band he gave me that night in Vegas.

"I don't need anything but you. We have video proof of that day, and who knows, maybe one day we might remember, but if not"—I shrug—"we have a lifetime of memories to make." I smile at him. "I just want to be yours."

He doesn't reply with words; instead, he shows me with his actions. His lips mold to mine, and he kisses me so tenderly it brings tears to my eyes. When he pulls away, I tear my shirt off over my head and reach for the button of my jean shorts.

"Brogan. We're outside."

"There is no one here, and the back patio is private."

"The lake," he reminds me.

"They can't see."

"What if they have binoculars?" he counters.

He's always looking out for me. "Fine, we'll use this." I grab the blanket I brought out with me because the nights still get cold. "Strip and sit down." He doesn't argue as he strips out of his shorts and boxer briefs, and then discards his shirt. He sits down on the lounger, and after I finish stripping, I straddle him, guiding him inside me.

"Home," I say, rocking my hips. I've lost count of the amount of times he's been inside me, but every single time, it feels like I'm coming home.

"I love you." He sits up and wraps the blanket over my shoulders and his arms around my waist, his lips trailing wet kisses over my collarbone and up my neck.

"I love you too." I smile when I think about the fact that he bought me an engagement ring, but I also have plans to give him a gift tonight. I wasn't sure how to go about giving it to him, but I think this is the perfect moment.

"So sweet," he says, nipping at my lips. His hands roam over every piece of skin he can reach, and I smile into his kiss.

"I have something for you too." I rock my hips, and he groans. I bite down on my lip to keep from crying out. Every time is better than the last.

"All I need is you," he says, lifting his hips.

"Oh, okay, so maybe I should go dig my birth control out of the trash," I say against his lips.

He freezes. "What?" He pulls back and we both stop moving as he stares into my eyes.

"You only need me, so that means we're putting making a baby on hold, right? So I should dig my pills out of the trash."

"You threw them away?"

I nod. "Yeah, I know it won't happen right away, but I thought maybe we could work on starting our family."

"You want to make a baby with me?" There are so many emotions and tenderness in his tone, but the one that stands out the most is happiness.

"I do. Do you want to make a baby with me?" I ask, even though I know the answer to that question.

"I do. I really fucking do." He laughs. "I never thought I could be this happy. I didn't know this kind of bliss existed until I met you."

"Did we just repeat our vows?" I tease.

"No. Yes. I don't know. What I do know is that I'm madly in love with you, and I want lots of babies."

"How about we start with one?" I chuckle.

"No way. We're going for twins." He grips my hips, lifts me the slightest bit, then pulls me back down. "Ride me, beautiful," he says as his thumb moves to rub over my clit.

I don't know if it's the intense conversation, the way he spoke to the night sky, pretending it was my father, the diamond ring he put on my finger, the fact that this very night we could potentially conceive our first baby, or if it's just him? Just Maddox, my husband. Whatever it is, it has me exploding around him, calling his name out to the night sky, and him quickly falling after me.

We stay connected as I snuggle under the blanket to his chest and watch as the final remnants of today's sunset disappears over the lake. It's a beautiful moment, one that I will cherish forever.

"Brogan?"

"Yeah?"

"When can we do that again?" he asks. He's smiling, and I hear the laughter in his tone. I have a feeling we're not going to get any rest until I'm knocked up.

"What about now?"

He doesn't answer. Instead, he moves to the edge of the lounger, stands with me in his arms, and carries me inside. Once we're in our room, he makes love to me for the second time tonight. He doesn't leave one area of skin untouched by his lips, and when we finish, we're both wearing matching grins.

Now.

This is our forever.

BROGAN EPILOGUE

One Month Later

"AUNT BROGAN!" RIVER, RAYNE, AND Lilly all come racing toward me.

I laugh because they see the red, white, and blue cupcakes I have in my hands. "Girls, do you want a cupcake?" I ask them. I'm not offended that they're happier to see the cupcakes than they are to see me.

"Yes!" they cheer.

They follow me to the table and take a seat. I help Lilly into a chair before I hand each one of them their cupcake. Lilly dives in, getting it all over her face, but she doesn't seem to mind as she grins, going in for another bite.

"She's messy." River giggles.

"But we're big girls, so we're not messy," Rayne says, as a big dollop of icing lands on her shirt.

"I think you're all messy," Maggie says, joining us.

"Hey, want a cupcake?" I ask her.

She waves me off. "No thanks. My belly hasn't been feeling the best."

"Daddy gives really good belly rubs," Rayne tells her. "When our bellies hurt."

Maggie chuckles. "I bet he does." Her eyes find mine, and we share a smile. The innocence of children.

"I have some upset stomach medicine in the hall bathroom cabinet. Help yourself," I tell Maggie.

"Thank you. I might have to take you up on that."

I sit beside her, watching the girls happily eat their treats. "So much has changed in a year," I tell Maggie.

"It has. But you look happy."

"I am happy. I didn't know I could be this happy," I tell her.

"All done!" River exclaims as she scrambles out of her chair, her sister hot on her heels. I intercept Lilly and wipe up her face, then call the girls back to do the same, before they head off to play.

"Next year, we'll have another," I muse.

"Just one?" Maggie asks.

"Maybe two," I admit. "We're trying, but I know these things take time."

"Are you kidding? The way your husband looks at you, I'm surprised we're all not pregnant." She snorts out a laugh.

"Who's pregnant?" Monroe asks as she, Emerson, and Briar join us.

"Just Briar, but I was telling Brogan that with the way Maddox looks at her, she won't be far behind. In fact, all of you"—Maggie waves her hand in the air—"are in great danger of being knocked up with the heated glances your husbands are tossing around like candy." She grins, and we all laugh.

She's not wrong.

"I'd be okay with that," Emerson speaks up.

"I guess Kane is close enough to one year," Monroe muses. "I want all of our kids to grow up together, and have a support system."

"Yeah," I agree.

"Maggie, what about you? Any new dating prospects?"

"Nope," she says, popping the *p*. "Dry as the Sahara Desert." Something flashes in her eyes, but it's gone too quickly to name.

"You'll find him," I tell her. "It happens when you least expect it."

"Amen," the ladies all chime in with their agreement.

"Meh, in the meantime, I'll live vicariously through all of you."

"Ladies," Lachlan says. He steps behind Maggie and places his hands on her shoulders, massaging gently. "What's going on over here? Talking about how handsome and charming I am? Go on, please proceed," he says, smirking.

"Actually, we were just telling Maggie we need to find her a man."

"What? You on the market, Mags?" he asks her. Something changes in his voice.

I study the two of them and the look that passes between them. I make a mental note to ask the ladies if they noticed it too. Maybe I'm so blinded by the love I have with Maddox, that I'm seeing things, but something... something is there.

"Nope," Maggie quips.

Lachlan bends and whispers something in her ear, and Maggie's face heats.

Interesting.

"Anyway, I think I'll take one of these." He snatches a cupcake out of the container, tears off the bottom half, places it on top—making a sandwich—and takes a huge bite. "So good," he mumbles. He shoves the second half into his mouth and reaches for another.

"How do you keep those abs with all that sugar you consume?" Emerson asks him.

He pulls up his shirt, pats his ripped abs, and grins. "You saying you think I'm sexy, Em?" he teases.

Emerson grabs a napkin, balls it up, and tosses it at him. "Don't let my husband hear you talk like that," she counters.

"Don't let me hear what, baby girl?" Roman asks.

"You better run, Lachlan," Monroe teases.

"What did you do to my wife?" Roman asks.

"Stole a cupcake," Lachlan says, reaching for another, but Maggie swats at his hand. "Hey." He pouts, but Maggie doesn't turn around to see it.

"What did we miss?" Forrest asks as he and Legend join us.

"Lachlan is eating all the cupcakes and flirting with Emerson," I tell them.

"That ring on her finger not reminder enough that she's mine?" Roman asks. He's joking, but there is something in his tone, a possessiveness that he's not bothering to hide where Emerson is concerned.

"We were talking about babies," Emerson says, gaining her husband's attention.

"Oh yeah?" Roman smiles down at his wife.

"That right there." Maggie points at them. "That's the look." The ladies all laugh, while the guys try to figure out what she's talking about.

"Maggie seems to think with the way you all look at us"—Briar waves her hand around in a circle—"that there could be a lot of new babies this time next year."

"I'm trying," Maddox says, making us all laugh.

Lilly comes toddling over, and Lachlan scoops her up in his arms. She rests her head on his shoulder. The familiarity hits me. This is what my kids are going to grow up knowing. Aunts and uncles who treat them like they are their own. So much love and support, something my sister and I had from one man.

I meet Briar's eyes, and she nods: she's reading my thoughts, and I know she's thinking the same thing. She's already experiencing it with River and Rayne.

This is our family.

I'm not sure if they chose us or we chose them, but we found each other, and I will be eternally grateful for having each and every one of them in our lives.

MADDOX
EPILOGUE

Two weeks later

It's a rainy Sunday afternoon. Brogan and I have been lounging most of the day. We finished a series we'd been watching, and now we're trying to figure out what to do next.

"I say we take a drive," Brogan suggests.

"Babe, it's nasty out there."

"Come on, old man," she teases. She stands and offers me her hand, and of course I take it. It doesn't matter where she wants to go, I'm damn sure going to follow her.

"Do we need something?" I ask her. We did our grocery shopping yesterday.

"Nope, just take a drive with me, husband."

"Let me grab my keys."

She smiles and rushes to slip her feet into her flip-flops. She's waiting for me by the door, and we walk out to my truck together. She darts off to her side of the truck and has the door open and slides inside before I even make it to my side. The rain has let up, so right now, it's just a drizzle, but it's still a dreary day. I'd much rather be snuggled up with my wife on our living room couch, but I can see whatever this little adventure is, it's something she really wants to do, so that's what we're doing.

"Right or left?" I ask her, as I idle at the end of our driveway.

"Let's go left." I do as she says as she messes with the radio, turning it to a country station and keeping the volume low. She sings softly to each new song that comes on. When I reach the stop sign in the center of town, I glance over at her.

"Left, right, or straight?"

"Hmm." She taps her index finger against her chin as if she's not sure, but I know my wife. She has a destination in mind. "Let's go right."

"Do I get a hint as to where I'm taking you?"

"Just a Sunday stroll," she says, but I can hear the smile in her voice. A quick glance over tells me that I'm right.

"What are you up to, Mrs. Lanigan?" I ask her.

"Why do I have to be up to something?" she asks.

"Because I know you."

"Fine," she relents. "I might have a destination in mind."

"Are you going to tell me where? I am the one driving, after all."

"Nah, you're doing a fine job. Take a right at the next stop sign."

"Are we going to the shop?" I ask her.

"We are," she confesses.

"Why are we going to the shop?"

"I want another tattoo."

"Really?" I ask, surprised. "You hadn't said anything. Do you know what you want?" I'm not gonna lie, the idea of putting more of my work on her soft skin lights a fire inside me. This is me. Being a tattoo artist is all I've ever wanted to do, and to have my wife accept my career so openly, even going as far as wanting her own ink, means more to me than she will ever know.

"I do."

"Are you going to tell me?" I laugh. "I mean, I am the guy doing the work, after all."

"I thought I could call Forrest, see if he wants...." Her voice trails off when my hand covers her mouth.

"Nope. None of that. Bad words, Brogan. So very bad." She's laughing so hard her entire body is shaking. She licks at my hand, and I pull it away from her mouth, wiping it on my shorts.

"I was just teasing. Of course I want it to be you. I'll tell you when we get there."

The rest of the drive to the shop is silent as I try hard to think about something she mentioned that she wanted. The only tattoo she ever said she wanted was the one she has. I'm certain of it.

"Here we are," I tell her, parking my truck. "Now, are you going to tell me?"

"Patience, my dear husband." She reaches for her handle, opens the door, and climbs out of the truck. I watch her as she walks toward the front door, and hovers under the awning waiting for me.

I let us inside, lock the door, and move down the dim hallway to my office. Inside, I flip on the light, and lean against my desk, arms crossed over my chest as I wait for her to tell me what's next.

"Can you do something for me?"

"Anything."

"Can you write our last name on a piece of paper?"

I furrow my brow in confusion, but do as she asks and hand it to her. She shakes her head. "You keep it."

"Why?"

"You need it for the stencil, right?"

"What?" I ask, but then her words register. "You want to get our name tattooed on you?"

"I do. In your handwriting."

The conversation from the day I gave Brogan her first tattoo filters through my mind. "Left bicep. Closest to your heart."

"Right where I want to always keep you."

"Come here." I pull her into my arms, and hug her so tightly I'm surprised she's able to breathe, but I just can't seem to help myself. This woman, she's my entire world, and I'll never be able to tell her what this means to me. Then again, maybe I can say it another way. Pulling my phone out of my pocket, I dial Lachlan.

"What's up?" he asks.

"Hey, can you meet me in the shop in about an hour?" I ask him.

"Sure. Everything okay?"

"Yeah, I just need some ink."

"Nice. I'll see you in an hour."

"Thanks, Lach." I end the call and shove my phone back into my pocket.

"What was that about?"

"I don't know how to tell you what this means to me. That you're putting a piece of me on you for a lifetime. The only way I can think of is to do the same. Lachlan will be here in an hour."

"Yeah? And where exactly are you going to put it?" she asks, her eyes roaming over my arms.

I tap my chest. "Right here, over my heart, where I want to keep you."

Her beaming smile lights not only the room, but me up inside. "I love you, Maddox."

"I love you too."

THANK YOU

for taking the time to read **What About Now?**
Want to read Lachlan's story?
Scan the QR code below to read, ***Can We Try?***

Never miss a new release:
Newsletter Sign-up

Be the first to hear about free content, new releases, cover reveals, sales, and more.
You can also find free reads and bonus content on my website.

CONTACT KAYLEE RYAN

Website:
kayleeryan.com/

Facebook:
bit.ly/2C5DgdF

Instagram:
instagram.com/kaylee_ryan_author/

Reader Group:
bit.ly/2o0yWDx

Goodreads:
bit.ly/2HodJvx

BookBub:
bit.ly/2KulVvH

TikTok:
tiktok.com/@kayleeryanauthor

More from Kaylee Ryan

With You Series:
Anywhere with You | More with You | Everything with You

Soul Serenade Series:
Emphatic | Assured | Definite | Insistent

Southern Heart Series:
Southern Pleasure | Southern Desire
Southern Attraction | Southern Devotion

Unexpected Arrivals Series
Unexpected Reality | Unexpected Fight | Unexpected Fall
Unexpected Bond | Unexpected Odds

Riggins Brothers Series:
Play by Play | Layer by Layer | Piece by Piece
Kiss by Kiss | Touch by Touch | Beat by Beat

Entangled Hearts Duet:
Agony | Bliss

Cocky Hero Club:
Lucky Bastard

More from Kaylee Ryan

Mason Creek Series:
Perfect Embrace

Standalone Titles:
Tempting Tatum | Unwrapping Tatum
Levitate | Just Say When
I Just Want You | Reminding Avery

Hey, Whiskey | Pull You Through | Remedy
The Difference | Trust the Push | Forever After All
Misconception | Never with Me | Merry with Me

Out of Reach Series:
Beyond the Bases | Beyond the Game
Beyond the Play | Beyond the Team

Kincaid Brothers Series:
Stay Always | Stay Over | Stay Forever | Stay Tonight
Stay Together | Stay Wild | Stay Present
Stay Anyway | Stay Real

Everlasting Ink Series:
Does He Know? | Is This Love? | Are You Ready?
What About Now? | Can We Try?

More from Kaylee Ryan

Co-written with Lacey Black:

Fair Lakes Series:
It's Not Over | Just Getting Started | Can't Fight It

Standalone Titles:
Boy Trouble | Home to You
Beneath the Fallen Stars | Beneath the Desert Sun
Tell Me A Story

Co-writing as Rebel Shaw with Lacey Black:
Royal | Crying Shame | Watch and Learn

There are so many people who are involved in the publishing process. I write the words, but I rely on my team of editors, proofreaders, and beta readers to help me make each book the best that it can be.

Those mentioned above are not the only members of my team. I have photographers, models, cover designers, formatters, bloggers, graphic designers, author friends, my PA, and so many more. I could not do this without these people.

And then there are my readers. If you're reading this, thank you. Your support means everything. Thank you for spending your hard-earned money on my words, and taking the time to read them. I appreciate you more than you know.

SPECIAL THANKS:

Becky Johnson, Hot Tree Editing.
Julie Deaton, Jo Thompson, and Jess Hodge, Proofreading
Lori Jackson Design – Model Cover
Emily Wittig Designs – Special Edition Cover
Michelle Lancaster – Photographer (Model Cover)
Chasidy Renee – Personal Assistant
Jamie, Stacy, Lauren, Franci, and Erica
Bloggers, Bookstagrammers, and TikTokers
Lacey Black and Kelly Elliott
Designs by Stacy and Ms. Betty – Graphics
The entire Give Me Books Team
The entire Grey's Promotion Team
My fellow authors
My amazing Readers

Printed in Great Britain
by Amazon